Peculiar

PENGUIN ⟨Ⓟ⟩ CLASSICS

A SENTIMENTAL JOURNEY

LAURENCE STERNE was born in 1713 at Clonmel, Ireland, the son of an army ensign. From 1723 until his father's death in 1731 he was sent to school in Halifax, Yorkshire, and in 1733 he entered as a sizar at Jesus College, Cambridge, receiving his BA in 1737. With the help of his uncle Jaques, precentor and canon at York, Sterne procured his livings. He took holy orders and in 1738 obtained the living of Sutton-on-the-Forest, near York, and a prebend in the cathedral. In 1741 he received the neighbouring benefice of Stillington and he was married, although his marriage was generally unhappy. Sterne wrote forty-five sermons, of which four volumes were published during his lifetime and three were published posthumously in 1769. His literary career began late and he wrote his first pamphlet, *A Political Romance*, in 1759, but it was suppressed because of its controversial satirical content. In the same year he began his masterpiece, *The Life and Opinions of Tristram Shandy*. The first two volumes made him a celebrity and he visited London, where he was lavishly fêted. Between 1761 and 1767 he brought out a further seven volumes. Sterne was dogged by ill health for much of his life and during his later years he alternated bouts of being lionized in London with recuperative continental travels and trips back to Yorkshire, where he always returned to write his next instalment. *A Sentimental Journey through France and Italy* represents Sterne's observations and experiences of two tours of the continent and is largely based on his time spent in France. The book was published in February 1768, barely three weeks before his death in London on 18 March 1768.

PAUL GORING is Senior Lecturer in British Literature at the Norwegian University of Science and Technology, Trondheim. His publications include *The Rhetoric of Sensibility in Eighteenth-Century Culture* (Cambridge University Press, 2005) and *Studying Literature* (co-authored; Arnold, 2001), as well as articles on Sterne, Virginia Woolf, and eighteenth-century drama, acting and elocution. He is also the editor of Penguin's forthcoming new edition of Samuel Johnson's *Rasselas*.

Capacity to replace event by feeling.

Like movements allow chance to operate

critique of egocentricism of sexually nationality, Yorick exposes himself to us — character in a falliable way

LAURENCE STERNE

A Sentimental Journey Through France and Italy by Mr. Yorick

With an Introduction and Notes by
PAUL GORING

PENGUIN BOOKS

PENGUIN BOOKS

Published by the Penguin Group
Penguin Books Ltd, 80 Strand, London WC2R 0RL, England
Penguin Group (USA) Inc., 375 Hudson Street, New York, New York 10014, USA
Penguin Books Australia Ltd, 250 Camberwell Road, Camberwell, Victoria 3124, Australia
Penguin Books Canada Ltd, 10 Alcorn Avenue, Toronto, Ontario, Canada M4V 3B2
Penguin Books India (P) Ltd, 11, Community Centre, Panchsheel Park, New Delhi – 110 017, India
Penguin Group (NZ), cnr Airborne and Rosedale Roads, Albany, Auckland 1310, New Zealand
Penguin Books (South Africa) (Pty) Ltd, 24 Sturdee Avenue, Rosebank 2196, South Africa

Penguin Books Ltd, Registered Offices: 80 Strand, London WC2R 0RL, England

www.penguin.com

First published 1768
This edition published in Penguin Classics 2001
Reprinted with updated Further Reading and corrections 2005
11

Introduction, Chronology and Notes copyright © Paul Goring, 2001, 2005
All rights reserved

The moral right of the editor has been asserted

Set in 10/12.5 pt Monotype Janson
Typeset by Rowland Phototypesetting Ltd, Bury St Edmunds, Suffolk
Printed in England by Clays Ltd, St Ives plc

ISBN-13: 978-0-14-043779-9

Contents

Acknowledgements

Throughout my work on this edition, I have benefited from the generous advice and assistance of many friends and scholars. For expert guidance on Sterne, I am grateful to Peter de Voogd, Peter Miles, Shaun Regan, David Shuttleton and, particularly, to Tom Keymer, who, as a previous editor of *A Sentimental Journey*, has been more than kind in offering ever-judicious advice. Many colleagues at Trondheim's English Department and Humanities Faculty have provided invaluable help and encouragement, among them Jeremy Hawthorn, Svein-Eirik Fauskevåg and Tone Midtgård. I am grateful to David Noy and Simon Meecham-Jones for sharing specialist expertise and for checking certain details, and to my father Michael Goring for his assiduous reading of drafts and for his stimulating suggestions. A grant from Trondheim's Humanities Faculty funded an assistant, Eli Løfaldli, who has helped me to prepare the text with an affable dedication beyond the call of duty. I would also like to thank the editors at Penguin with whom it has been a pleasure to produce this edition.

Paul Goring

Chronology

1713   (24 November) born at Clonmel, Ireland, the second child and first son of Agnes Sterne and Roger Sterne, an army ensign.

1723   Sent to grammar school near Halifax, Yorkshire.

1731   Death of father.

1733   Enters Jesus College, Cambridge.

1737   Receives BA degree;
takes holy orders;
becomes assistant curate of St Ives, near Cambridge.

1738   Becomes assistant curate of Catton, Yorkshire;
is ordained as priest;
becomes vicar of Sutton-on-the-Forest, near York.

1740   Receives MA degree.

1741   Appointed prebendary of York Minster;
marries Elizabeth Lumley and settles at Sutton;
contributes essays to pro-Walpole York newspaper.

1743   Publishes poem, 'The Unknown World', in the *Gentleman's Magazine*.

1744   Gains second church living of Stillington, near Sutton;
purchases farm land.

1745   First daughter Lydia is born and dies.

1747   Preaches and publishes charity sermon, 'The Case of Elijah';
birth of second daughter Lydia.

1750   Preaches and publishes 'The Abuses of Conscience'.

1751   Appointed Commissary of the Peculiar Court of Pickering and Pocklington.

1756   Gains land from Sutton Enclosure Act;
Seven Years War begins.

1759   (January) *A Political Romance* is printed and withdrawn;

writes 'Fragment in the Manner of Rabelais';

death of mother;

(December) *The Life and Opinions of Tristram Shandy, Gentleman* I–II published in York;

liaison with Kitty Fourmantel, a singer (whose friendship with David Garrick Sterne exploits to promote *Tristram Shandy* in London).

1760   *Tristram Shandy* celebrated in London;

(March) travels to London and is lionized;

(May) publishes *The Sermons of Mr. Yorick* I–II;

(May) returns to Yorkshire and new living at Coxwold;

moves into 'Shandy Hall'.

1761   (January) publishes *Tristram Shandy* III–IV;

(December) publishes *Tristram Shandy* V–VI.

1762   Travels to France (England and France still technically at war);

is celebrated in Paris;

travels south.

1763   In Toulouse and Montpellier with wife and daughter;

meets Tobias Smollett;

Treaty of Paris ends Seven Years War.

1764   (May) returns to England, leaving wife and daughter in France.

1765   (January) publishes *Tristram Shandy* VII–VIII;

(October) leaves for the Continent and travels in France and Italy for eight months.

1766   (January) *The Sermons of Mr. Yorick* III–IV published;

(May) Tobias Smollett's *Travels through France and Italy* published;

(June) returns to England; preaches his last sermon.

1767   (January) publishes *Tristram Shandy* IX;

(April) falls in love with Mrs Elizabeth Draper, who leaves for India to join her husband;

writes *The Journal to Eliza* (published posthumously);

writes *A Sentimental Journey*.

1768   (27 February) publishes *A Sentimental Journey* I–II;

(18 March) dies in London;

buried at St George's, Hanover Square.

1769   *Sermons by the Late Rev. Mr. Sterne* V–VII published by Lydia Sterne.

1773   *Letters from Yorick to Eliza* published;
        Elizabeth Sterne dies.

1775   *Letters of the Late Rev. Mr. Laurence Sterne* (including other works) published.

1904   *The Journal to Eliza* first published in *The Works and Life of Laurence Sterne*.

1969   Sterne's bones reburied at Coxwold.

Introduction

'I have laid a plan for something new, quite out of the beaten track', wrote Laurence Sterne to his daughter early in 1767.[1] A year later, the work was published and it was indeed something new on the literary scene. Narrated by Yorick, an impulsive traveller who sets off for France on a whim, *A Sentimental Journey through France and Italy* is a captivating and intriguing story of an Englishman's experiences abroad, and it has fascinated readers ever since its appearance in London in 1768. Sterne's hero follows a route that would have been fairly typical for eighteenth-century British tourists – he travels south from Calais, through Paris and towards the Italian border – but *A Sentimental Journey* is no conventional tourist's account of a newly experienced land. Early on, Yorick proudly explains that 'my travels and observations will be altogether of a different cast from any of my fore-runners' (p. 13), and the fictional travelogue that follows is certainly a distinctive and idiosyncratic work. Shifting rapidly from scene to scene, *A Sentimental Journey* jolts the reader through a hectic succession of Yorick's anecdotes, experiences and observations, and the bumpiness of this narrative journey is matched by Yorick's abrupt, conversational manner of address.

The main focus of the fiction falls upon the minutiae of Yorick's response to foreign experience, and Sterne is rarely concerned to document outward details of the journey itself. *A Sentimental Journey* is thus very much an inward voyage into the emotional life of the central character and narrator, and it is doubtless this intimate psychological focus which, together with a strong thread of comedy, has sustained the work's appeal among both novel readers and later novelists. As a 'sentimental' traveller, Yorick is given to displaying sympathy and charity towards those he meets en route, and this sensitivity has caused many readers to find in the story a rich vein of pathos. But Yorick's sentimentality can sometimes appear insincere or compromised by sensual interest, and other readers have been shocked or amused by the erotic predicaments that Yorick seems perpetually to fall into and by the dubious innocence with which he explains such events. Still other readers have been left unsure quite how to respond to this narrative which, exhibiting a masterly control of subtle ambiguity, repeatedly and remarkably seems to disclose information that runs counter to Yorick's version of events. As Sterne was writing the work, he assured his bookseller Thomas Becket that his latest offering was 'likely to take in all Kinds of Readers'[2] – *A Sentimental Journey* has succeeded in doing exactly that.

Sterne's Literary Career and His Fictional Guises[3]

A Sentimental Journey was Sterne's second and final major work of fiction, written in his last year and cut short by his death. It was the work of a man who had already made his name as an author and had gained a reputation for a decidedly playful attitude to literary convention and decorum. Born in Ireland in 1713, Sterne had attended school in Yorkshire and in 1733 had entered Jesus College, Cambridge. He took holy orders in 1737 and spent most of his working life as the vicar of two rural Yorkshire parishes and as a prebendary of York Minster. He was married (not altogether happily) with one daughter, and for twenty years he led a relatively obscure clerical life punctuated by occasional authorial ventures. He had published two sermons, a poem, some political journalism and a political satire before his literary career really took off, late in 1759, with *The Life and Opinions of Tristram Shandy, Gentleman*. When the first two volumes of this witty and notoriously odd pseudo-autobiography were sold in London, *Tristram Shandy* became a phenomenal success and its popularity soon established Sterne as an international literary celebrity. It was a status he had hoped for – 'I wrote not [to] be *fed*, but to be *famous*',[4] he told a correspondent in 1760.

The main point of *Tristram Shandy* is to dramatize, in a comical and digressive manner, the difficulties of shaping into narrative form the infinite raw and disorganized details that make up an individual's life. Tristram attempts to write his autobiography, but with the material of his life swelling impossibly beyond his authorial control, his narrative becomes as much a commentary upon the activity of writing as a rendering of his life itself. For both Sterne and his constantly frustrated narrator, life writing was an enterprise that would inevitably expand, and over the years that followed *Tristram Shandy*'s initial triumph Sterne added to the work. He had prepared the way for continuation in the first instalment – Tristram resolves 'not to be in a hurry;---but to go on leisurely, writing and publishing two volumes of my life every year'.[5] These fictional intentions were followed (albeit loosely) by Sterne, who by 1767 had written a further seven volumes. Critics continue to debate whether Sterne had actually finished *Tristram Shandy* when he reached the end of the ninth volume – the issue is problematic largely because, with a deliberately unconventional chronology and a characteristically digressive manner of progression, the work moves towards no typical endpoint. Its 'great humour', as Horace Walpole identified it, 'consists in the whole narration always going backwards',[6] an effect which stems from Tristram's aspirations to explain fully the circumstances behind his being. His method is 'to come at the first springs of the events I tell',[7] such that he rarely arrives at telling the events themselves. Tristram is not born until the fourth volume and, apart from a few sparse references to his adult life, only his infant self appears in the action. The bulk of *Tristram Shandy* is taken up with Tristram's humorous philosophical reflections, bawdy anecdotes and comic stories of his eccentric family.

Tristram Shandy is very different from *A Sentimental Journey* but it nevertheless contains many features which Sterne would reuse or develop for the later work. Both works are dominated by deeply self-conscious narrators, and the manner of telling often becomes as prominent a focus of interest as the matter being told. Sterne's narrators also share a ready willingness to digress, whether it be for the inclusion of an anecdote, a fragment of a story or a passage of philosophical musing. In addition, both works are jokingly self-conscious about the physical nature of printed literature: *Tristram Shandy* is laden with typographical playfulness, with misplaced chapters and missing pages, with an entirely black page, a marbled page and a blank page, and with numerous other devices which draw attention to the materiality of literary fiction. This strain of humour is less developed in *A Sentimental Journey*, but is nonetheless apparent in the eccentric repetition of chapter headings, in Yorick's writing of his preface several chapters into the work and in the suggestively unpunctuated concluding sentence. Sterne had furthermore explored in *Tristram Shandy* many of the subjects that clearly engage Yorick – the subtle nature of flirtation, for example, and the role of the body and its gestures in social interaction – and he also drew from the earlier work for his cast of characters. Tristram himself, his father, Walter, and his benevolent Uncle Toby are all mentioned in *A Sentimental Journey*, but perhaps the most significant continuity between the two works lies in the character of Yorick, who had a pre-existence among the *dramatis personae* of Tristram's life before becoming the central voice of Sterne's final work.

For many of Sterne's early readers, a preconceived sense of Yorick's identity would have significantly informed their experience of *A Sentimental Journey*, and it is worth examining the public status of 'Yorick' so as to restore some sense of how the text related to its narrator's established image. Yorick appears throughout *Tristram Shandy*'s nine volumes, although with Sterne's typical handling of narrative chronology his death is recounted in the first. (In fact, paradoxically, according to the internal logic of Sterne's fiction, Yorick is dead before he even sets out for France!) Yorick is the Shandy family's local clergyman, and is so named, Tristram records, because of his lineal descent from the Yorick of *Hamlet*, 'the king's chief Jester'.[8] Sterne's Yorick is marked by his ancestor's profession: he is forever 'scattering his wit and his humour,—his gibes and his jests about him',[9] and in this way Yorick was, at least in part, a portrait of Sterne himself. Sterne greatly admired and emulated Rabelais and Swift, both clergymen and comic writers whose church positions did little to thwart their production of bawdy satires. Sterne similarly adopted and enjoyed a position as a 'laughing cleric', and having created such a figure in Yorick, he publicly encouraged the projection of this character's identity back upon himself. Indeed, Sterne continually blurred the boundary between himself and his fiction – he cultivated his persona as 'Tristram', he named his house 'Shandy Hall' – such that 'Sterne', 'Tristram' and 'Yorick' became often interchangeable terms. Walpole wrote of 'Sterne's sentimental travels';[10] obituaries of Sterne mourned 'Yorick' and 'Tristram'.[11]

Sterne's personal elision with 'Yorick' was particularly thorough-going. He had incorporated one of his own sermons into *Tristram Shandy*, where it appears as written by Yorick, and in 1760 he capitalized on *Tristram Shandy*'s vogue by publishing *The Sermons of Mr. Yorick*, a two-volume compilation of sermons he had written for his services in Yorkshire. It was a manœuvre which brought both sales and scandal. The eighteenth-century book trade thrived on moral, didactic litera-ture, and collections of sermons comprised a vital part of the industry; but rarely would these serious works appear pseudonymously, least of all when the pseudonym called to mind a 'fellow of infinite jest'. Sterne's apparent flouting of Anglican sobriety was appalling to some: 'Would any man believe that a Preacher was in earnest, who should mount the pulpit in a *Harlequin's coat*?' wrote the outraged critic of the *Monthly Review*.[12] Nevertheless *The Sermons* appealed to the public. There were numerous new editions and with the addition of two more volumes in 1766, the name and identity of Yorick were well established in the public consciousness by the time of *A Sentimental Journey*. 'Yorick' also served Sterne's amorous ends, and was the face for his 'sentimental' affair of 1767 with Mrs Elizabeth Draper, much of it conducted in an epistolary journal 'wrote under the fictitious Names of Yorick & Draper'.[13]

As a character in *Tristram Shandy*, as a semi-autobiographical mask for Sterne and as a pseudo-author of sermons, 'Yorick' was a pliable mixture of fact and fiction, of seriousness and frivolity, of Christian virtue and humorous indulgence. And in *A Sentimental Journey* – which, like *The Sermons*, was offered to the public as authored *By Mr. Yorick* – the tensions in the personality are sustained and compounded. In the text itself, Yorick's clerical profession is signalled explicitly by only a couple of passing references (they can easily be missed), but Yorick nonetheless seems often to be fulfilling the position of a chaste and worthy clergyman. He regularly adopts a highly sermonizing tone; he lards his tale with biblical allusions and quotations; and he is careful to declare his purity of body and mind. Yet, while Yorick is no longer quite the brazen jester of *Tristram Shandy*, his insistently 'innocent' narrative is nevertheless shot through with innuendoes and with strong hints that Yorick's real interests are as much sexual as they are senti-mental. With Yorick's final public appearance, then, Sterne advanced the complexity of the personality he had created, and retained his ability to cause scandal. Indeed, for Joseph Cockfield, an early reader of *A Sentimental Journey*, Sterne's literary conduct was becoming more shocking than ever: 'in his former writings I saw evident marks of his genius and benevolence, but who that indulges serious reflection can read his obscenity and ill-applied passages of Holy Scripture, without horror!'[14]

Alongside profession and personality, the later Yorick also shared with his author a keen interest in travel. Sterne may have written for fame rather than fortune, but he pursued the latter nonetheless and he enjoyed the new opportunities that literary success brought him. With the proceeds from *Tristram Shandy* and *The Sermons*, Sterne was able to make two trips to the Continent, and to pay a curate to attend to his parish duties while he was away. He was a long-standing sufferer from consumption – at Cambridge he had 'bled the bed full' from a broken vessel in his lungs[15] – and, like many travellers of the time, he was in search of better health when he migrated to the warmer south. His first trip, beginning in January 1762, took him to Paris where, preceded by his reputation, he was welcomed in the fashionable and intellectual salons (Yorick would also visit them). From Paris he travelled south and stayed with his wife and daughter in Toulouse and Montpellier, before returning to England in June 1764. He was on the road again in October 1765, this time to tour Italy, where he visited Turin, Milan, Florence, Rome and Naples, before returning to England via Paris in June 1766. Sterne's experiences abroad clearly provided inspiration and material for his writing, but just as he transformed aspects of himself to create Tristram and Yorick, so too did he fictionalize his travels.

A Sentimental Journey was Sterne's second experiment in travel writ-ing. He first made literary capital from his travels in Volume VII of *Tristram Shandy*, which appeared in January 1765. Quite unlike the other volumes, with their mostly Yorkshire settings, Volume VII presents Tristram on a whistle-stop tour of France. His travels echo Sterne's first health-seeking journey through France. Tristram, sharing his creator's 'vile cough', is fleeing 'DEATH himself', who comes knocking on his door and interrupts him in the middle of telling a bawdy story.[16] It is fitting that Death should disrupt an act of narration: Tristram is living faster than he can write and his life-story is doomed to be interrupted finally by his death. Here, though, Tristram resolves to lead Death 'a dance he little thinks of . . . if he follows me, I pray God he may break his neck'.[17] Tristram does outwit Death and he survives to write two more volumes of his story. It was not an example that Sterne followed. He had planned *A Sentimental Journey* as 'a new work of four volumes' and he had gathered subscriptions for a work of that length.[18] But Sterne was ill in the summer and autumn of 1767, and it became apparent that only the first two volumes would be ready for the winter (Sterne's preferred season for publication). These two volumes were published on 27 February 1768, and, less than three weeks later, on 18 March, Sterne's 'vile cough' caught up with him and he died. Yorick's journey '*through France and Italy*' was curtailed before he had reached the Italian border, and the narrative was interrupted for ever in the middle of a particularly bawdy story.

Sterne and Eighteenth-century Travel Literature

Travelling to Europe for pleasure or for health had become in the eighteenth century an increasingly popular pursuit for the British educated and moneyed classes, and the book market catered plentifully for this expanding interest. A genre of travel literature was well established by the beginning of the century, and travel accounts and practical guidebooks remained a staple of the publishing industry throughout Sterne's lifetime and beyond. Works such as Joseph Addison's *Remarks on Several Parts of Italy* (1705), John Breval's *Remarks on Several Parts of Europe* (1726) and Thomas Nugent's *The Grand Tour* (1749) satisfied the needs and interests of men and women planning tours, of returned travellers and of readers keen to know more of the world beyond Britain but without the means to travel themselves.[19]

Sterne's fictional travel writing engages with this literary field and displays his characteristically wry approach to literary convention. He used the opportunity to satirize the existing genre, and thus he self-consciously staked the position of his own work in relation to other publications which he found ridiculous, disagreeable or simply convenient foils for his own wit. Volume VII of *Tristram Shandy* wholeheartedly mocks the genre – it would be, Sterne puffed in a letter, 'a laughing good temperd Satyr against Travelling'[20] – and it derides typical travel accounts as predictable, tedious, bound by convention and, in many cases, bogus. Tristram makes clear the difference of his own narrative practices: '"NOW before I quit Calais," a travel-writer would say, "it would not be amiss to give some account of it."—Now I think it very much amiss—that a man cannot go quietly through a town, and let it alone, when it does not meddle with him.'[21] *A Sentimental Journey* similarly stresses its distance from the generic norm. When Yorick categorizes travellers in his preface, he asserts his uniqueness as a 'Sentimental Traveller', suggesting his entitlement in 'the whole circle of travellers' to a 'nitch entirely to myself' (pp. 12–13). He eschews both the style of conventional travel writing and the matter with which it is typically concerned. If Yorick seeks to reveal 'the precise and distinguishing marks of national characters' (a common theme of travel writing), he discovers them more in 'nonsensical *minutiæ*', such as a barber's choice of a metaphor, 'than in the most important matters of state' (p. 48). When he visits the Paris opera, his attention is caught not, as might be expected, by the performance or the architecture, but by the characters in the audience. For Ralph Griffiths, writing in the *Monthly Review* in April 1768, Yorick's conspicuous unconcern with the usual tourist attractions was a refreshing novelty: '*ordinary travellers*', he wrote, 'would have told us how many statues and pictures they met with in their visit to the capital of France; and who chizel'd the one, and who pencil'd the other: but the genius of Yorick was superior to such uninteresting details'.[22] Sterne's engagement with travel literature, then, was seen as no hollow attack upon a genre he found unsatisfactory, but rather as the foundation of a new way of writing about foreign experience.

A Sentimental Journey's satire of travel literature is pointed above all towards one particular work: Tobias Smollett's *Travels through France and Italy*. In fact, the usual abridgement of *A Sentimental Journey through France and Italy* to the more convenient and more novelistic *A Sentimental Journey* has tended to veil what is a fairly explicit allusion to Smollett's title. Smollett, a Scot who had given up an unsuccessful medical career to become a novelist and critic, had travelled on the Continent, like Sterne, in search of health (the two met in Montpellier). He wrote an account of his journey in the form of letters back to England, and it was published in May 1766, while Sterne was returning from Italy. It is difficult to describe Smollett's *Travels* without being swayed by the harsh condemnation which appears in *A Sentimental Journey* – indeed Sterne's powerful critique has coloured the reception of the work for ever. Nevertheless, it is probably fair to say that Smollett's work is bad-tempered, acerbic, xenophobic, filled with complaint and generally expressive of a deep resistance to foreign cultures. 'I hate the French cookery, and abominate garlick,' he wrote in one of his lighter moments.[23] Some later critics, seeking to redeem the *Travels*, have argued that the narrator should be seen not as Smollett but as a fictional character,[24] but whatever the relation between the narrative voice and the real Smollett, the work represented an epitome of ill-humour abroad, and it was as such that Sterne exploited it.

Sterne alluded dismissively to Smollett's travels in the last volume of *Tristram Shandy*: 'I do not think a journey through France and Italy, provided a man keeps his temper all the way, so bad a thing as some people would make you believe.'[25] Tristram suggests that the goodness of a journey depends fundamentally upon the character and mood of the traveller, not upon the convenience or stimulation provided within the foreign land. This critique is developed in *A Sentimental Journey*, in which Sterne invoked Smollett's *Travels* to represent all the things his own work wouldn't be. He alludes to Smollett several times and provides an obvious caricature in 'the learned SMELFUNGUS', who sets out on his travels 'with the spleen and jaundice, and every object he pass'd by was discoloured or distorted—He wrote an account of them, but 'twas nothing but the account of his miserable feelings' (p. 28). Such a use of Smollett (doubtless an embellished and partial one) was important to Sterne's project because it enabled him to draw a distinction between two very different ways of responding to the foreign: one where the encounter with the unfamiliar is determined by a rigid self; the other where the self is receptive to definition by the unfamiliar. Smollett finds the Continent ghastly, Sterne's work suggests, because 'every object' is yellowed through his fixed and jaundiced gaze. Sterne's narrator, on the other hand, is susceptible to transformation by his environment and indeed is eager to chart the internal 'ebbs and flows of our humours' (p. 7). Yorick insists that he is 'govern'd by circumstances—I cannot govern them' (p. 76), and his account is partially the record of his watching himself respond to the world around him. He records, for example, how he is unable *not* to hire his servant La Fleur (whose skills stretch no further than basic drumming) because 'the genuine look and air of the fellow determined the matter at once in his favour' (p. 31).

Yorick's receptivity gives him a toleration of difference which further distinguishes him from Smelfungus. Set against the gallophobia of Smollett's *Travels*, Yorick's famous opening sentence – 'THEY order, said I, this matter better in France' (p. 5) – stands out as a bold assertion of unprejudiced tolerance. Whatever 'this matter' is (we never find out, and the vagueness allows the phrase to resound generally) the French are ungrudgingly attributed with superior skills in its ordering. The opening scenes further dramatize the notion that fulfilling travel depends upon a traveller with tolerance and a willingness to adapt. Yorick, having given short shrift to a mendicant monk, regrets his discourtesy and resolves to 'learn better manners as I get along' (p. 10). A traveller like Smelfungus knows what he likes and knows what good manners are before he sets out; Yorick is prepared to rediscover such things along the way.

Is that what it means to travel sentimentally?

Sentiment and Sentimental Literature[26]

'Sentimental' was a relatively new term when Sterne was writing. Its first recorded use is in a letter of 1749 from Lady Bradshaigh to the novelist Samuel Richardson. 'What, in your opinion', she asked him, 'is the meaning of the word *sentimental*, so much in vogue amongst the polite, both in town and country?' and her letter goes on to describe the modish currency of this freshly minted term despite its apparently unsettled meaning:

Every thing clever and agreeable is comprehended in that word ... I am frequently astonished to hear such a one is a *sentimental* man; we were a *sentimental* party; I have been taking a *sentimental* walk. And that I might be reckoned a little in the fashion, and, as I thought, show them the proper use of the word, about six weeks ago, I declared I had just received a *sentimental* letter.[27]

For the Methodist preacher John Wesley, the term still lacked proper meaning in 1772: '*Sentimental*! what is that?' he complained when confronted with Sterne's book. 'It is not sense,' he went on. 'It conveys no determinate idea ... And this nonsensical word ... is becoming a fashionable one.'[28] 'Sentiment' was more widely comprehended than the adjective it spawned, but, as Sterne himself recognized, here too there was no firm agreement regarding its meaning, at least not among the French: 'notwithstanding they make such a pother about the *word*,' he wrote in a letter of 1765, 'they have no precise idea annex'd to it'.[29] There was, then, a web of confusing meanings (and non-meanings) surrounding the fashionable vocabulary of sentimentalism, but it is nevertheless possible to isolate certain threads of near consensus.

'Sentiment' was generally used to mean a thought or a reflection which was produced from or informed by emotion; it conveyed a 'mental feeling' – an attitude which is at once intellectual and emotional, and typically this attitude concerned moral conduct. It is in such a sense that Adam Smith used the term in his *Theory of Moral Sentiments* (1759), which argues that proper conduct in society depends upon the exercise of *sympathy* for one's fellow beings; a rational moral system is discovered firstly by emotional impulse. Samuel Richardson applied the term in the same way – indeed it was appropriate that Lady Bradshaigh should consult Richardson on the matter, for the promotion of 'sentiments' in this sense was the very *raison d'être* of his novels. In *Pamela* (1740), *Clarissa* (1747–8) and *Sir Charles Grandison* (1753–4), Richardson endeavoured to arouse readers' emotions for the purposes of moral instruction. Typically he created affecting scenes of distress depicting virtuous characters suffering at the hands of villainy. His fiction aims to arouse readers' sympathies for the victim, and thus, through inviting their emotional identification, to instil in readers a 'natural' sense of justice and of proper conduct. It was this intended 'product' of Richardson's novels that Samuel Johnson recognized as 'sentiment' when he famously urged that one must read Richardson 'for the sentiment, and consider the story as only giving occasion to the sentiment'.[30] In fact, if readers needed a short-cut through the story, they could consult Richardson's *A Collection of ... Moral and Instructive Sentiments* (1755), a user-friendly compilation of didactic extracts from the three novels.

'Sentimental', therefore, did not have the pejorative sense of 'excessively emotional' or 'mawkish' that it has since acquired. When applied to things – Lady Bradshaigh's letter, Yorick's journey – it suggested 'capable of generating sentiments' or perhaps 'likely to put a sensitive individual in a mood of moral reflection'. When applied to people, it implied their capacity to feel sympathy for others and, consequently, their desire to alleviate the suffering of others. Being 'sentimental', or possessing 'sensibility' (an important related term which is used in *A Sentimental Journey*), was a sign of innate goodness; it was an expression of an individual's unique capacity to *feel* virtue. Explained in physiological terms, a sentimental capacity was seen as a privilege of the few whose nerves and fibres were attuned to a degree of hypersensitivity. The physician George Cheyne, author of the popular medical treatise *The English Malady* (1733), asserted that 'there are as many and as different Degrees of *Sensibility* or of *Feeling*, as there are degrees of *Intelligence* and Perception in *human* Creatures'.[31] As such, a fine sensibility was a quality that many individuals sought to display, and an important function of sentimental literature was that it enabled them to do so. An article of 1796 in the *Monthly Magazine* recalled a time 'when sensibility was taken under the patronage of that powerful arbiter of manners – fashion. Then, height of breeding was measured by delicacy of feeling, and no fine lady, or gentleman, was ashamed to be seen sighing over a pathetic story, or weeping at a deep-wrought tragedy.'[32]

Sentimentalism penetrated all literary genres in the eighteenth century, and following the influential example of Richardson, it had a marked effect upon prose fiction. From the 1740s, there appeared a rash of novels which, with their emotional characters and distressing stories, provided readers with ample opportunities to sympathize with suffering and thus to exercise and display their own capacities for sentiment. Some, such as Sarah Fielding's *David Simple* (1744 and 1753) and Henry Brooke's *The Fool of Quality* (1764–70), endeavoured to maintain the moral drive of Richardson's work. In others, such as Henry Mackenzie's *The Man of Feeling* (1771), sentimentality became more indulgently lachrymose, and less emphasis was placed upon the supposed didactic function of pathos. Throughout the genre, stock characters and conventional situations were deployed to stir the emotions of readers: delicate heroes and heroines perform selfless acts of charity; the sick groan meekly through extenuated illness; virtuous lovers weep at separation and reunion; characters are lost for words as a language of tearful gesture takes over to convey their heightened emotions.

The genre became sufficiently formulaic to provoke satire of its conventions. Late in the century, Mary Alcock facetiously offered advice to the would-be novelist in a long verse *Receipt for Writing a Novel* (1799), and she hardly exaggerated the reality of sentimental fiction when she prescribed the ingredients:

> Hysteric fits at least a score,
> Or, if you find occasion, more;
> But fainting-fits you need not measure,
> The fair ones have them at their pleasure;
> Of sighs and groans take no account,
> But throw them in to vast amount.[33]

Furthermore, the motives and morality of sentimental fiction had been subject to scepticism and attack from its earliest years. In 1741, Henry Fielding had expressed a deep suspicion of sentimentalism in *Shamela*, a parodic reworking of *Pamela* which ridiculed Richardson's literary style and sought to expose sentimental virtue as a cover for go-getting self-interest. And indeed, throughout its vogue, sentimental literature was sometimes caught up within combative cultural debate. Sterne's sentimental writing occupies a particularly delicate position within that debate. Indeed, the most enduring issue in critical arguments surrounding *A Sentimental Journey* has been the degree to which sincerity or mockery ultimately underlies the work's participation in sentimental culture. Thackeray asserted his mistrust of Sterne's sentiment in his *Lectures on the English Humourists* of 1851, asking: 'How much was deliberate calculation and imposture—how much was false sensibility—and how much true feeling? Where did the lie begin, and did he know where? and where did the truth end in the art and scheme of this man of genius, this actor, this quack?'[34] Nuanced versions of such questions have remained central throughout twentieth-century criticism of *A Sentimental Journey*. Numerous studies have been preoccupied with, as one critic puts it, the text's 'ambiguous teetering between appeals for sentimental identification and displays of ironic, witty distance' and with the question of 'whether Yorick's encounters have a predatory, exploitive dimension that undercuts their evocations of fine feeling'.[35] And it is because ambiguity is so fundamental to Sterne's method that such questions will continue to be asked.

Sentiment and Suggestion

From the earliest instalment of *Tristram Shandy*, there had been a sentimental strain in Sterne's work. Pathos mingles often with the comedy – indeed, Tristram's history is largely a succession of lamentable misfortunes. Sterne amplified the sentimental aspect of *Tristram Shandy* as it developed, and from the flashes of sentiment in the early volumes, he began to develop extended scenes of highly charged pathos. They won him considerable approval: a celebrated episode in Volume VI charting the death of Le Fever, a 'poor sick lieutenant',[36] was, for the *Critical Review*, 'beautifully pathetic' with material to appeal 'to every reader of sensibility'.[37] Of the same passage, the *Monthly Review* concluded that Sterne's 'excellence lay not so much in the humorous as in the pathetic', and the reviewer was pleased also to see Sterne moderating the bawdy content of his writing.[38] Reviewing Volumes VII and VIII for the *Monthly Review* in 1765, Ralph Griffiths echoed this selective approval, and indeed urged Sterne to cultivate a new project where he might focus more purely upon the sentimental:

Suppose you were to strike out a new plan? Give us none but amiable or worthy, or exemplary characters; or, if you will, to enliven the drama, throw in the *innocently humorous* ... Paint Nature in her loveliest dress—her native simplicity. Draw natural scenes, and interesting situations—In fine, Mr. Shandy, do, for surely you can, excite our passions to *laudable* purposes— awake our affections, engage our hearts—arouze, transport, refine, improve us. Let morality, let the cultivation of virtue be your aim—let wit, humour, elegance and pathos be the means; and the grateful applause of mankind will be your reward.[39]

Whether influenced by the review or not, Sterne's development as a writer lay in the directions Griffiths sketched. The final instalment of *Tristram Shandy* was a single short volume – Sterne's letters suggest he was eager to be getting on with what would become *A Sentimental Journey* before continuing 'Tristram with fresh spirit'[40] – and as he wrote it he was tapping his sentimental vein. In particular, Volume IX includes a return to Tristram's journey through France and his emotional encounter with the 'poor hapless' Maria of Moulins, an abandoned virgin and, for Tristram and many readers, a most eloquent object of pity.[41] Maria would be visited by Yorick towards the end of the later work, and it seems almost as though Sterne was experimenting and making preparations for *A Sentimental Journey* as he wrote what would be *Tristram Shandy*'s last volume.

Sterne's progress with *A Sentimental Journey* is mentioned in various of his letters, several of which further suggest that, like Ralph Griffiths, he had come to favour the sentimental side of his literary personality. To certain of his correspondents, he was clearly keen to parade his new work as the sincere outpouring of a sensitive 'man of feeling'. In September 1767, he told a friend, 'my Sentimental Journey will, I dare say, convince you that my feelings are from the heart, and that that heart is not of the worst of molds—praised be God for my sensibility!'[42] In November 1767, we find him assuring a respectable female friend that his 'Sentimental Journey ... is a subject which works well, and suits the frame of mind I have been in for some time past—I told you my design in it was to teach us to love the world and our fellow creatures better than we do—so it runs most upon those gentler passions and affections, which aid so much to it.'[43] This tenderly didactic writing, he assures, is the work of a man in a new 'frame of mind' – it is as though he is putting his associations with *Tristram Shandy* behind him so as to reveal a purer sentimentalist within. He seeks more explicitly to negate the brand of Tristram in a letter later that month to an unnamed Earl. He thanks him for a 'letter of enquiry about Yorick' and reports:

he has worn out both his spirits and his body with the Sentimental Journey— 'tis true that an author must feel himself, or his reader will not—but I have torn my whole frame into pieces by my feelings … I have long been a sentimental being—whatever your Lordship may think to the contrary.— The world has imagined, because I wrote Tristram Shandy, that I was myself more Shandean than I really ever was.[44]

Anxious to refute his public image as a flippant and bawdy humorist, he promotes the new work as the occasion when the real Sterne will drop the mask of Tristram and come forth upon the page emotionally naked. *A Sentimental Journey* would be, a friend reported Sterne claiming, 'his *Work of Redemption*'.[45]

But the motivation behind Sterne's sentimentalism demands a more cynical view – or, at least, a more complicated one. Considering his opportunism and interest in maintaining sales, his sentimental turn might easily be seen as a shrewd response to the public's changing attitude to his fiction. When Ralph Griffiths urged Sterne to pursue his sentimental writing, he also suggested that the public were tiring of *Tristram Shandy* and 'will have *had enough*, by the time they get to the end of your eighth volume'[46] – and it is true that sales of *Tristram Shandy* were dropping off. Sterne was certainly keen to restore his popularity and he was clearly delighted when his proposed new work was attracting a healthy flow of subscriptions – in February 1767, we find him boasting to his banker in Paris that it 'will bring me a thousand guineas (au moins)'.[47] Sterne may have 'long been a sentimental being', but he was also undeniably interested in what his sentiments were worth.

Perhaps more significantly, though, other of Sterne's letters hint that his attitude to sentimentalism was not nearly as pure or as free from satiric impulse as he elsewhere sought to advertise. A letter of December 1767 to George Macartney, a diplomat Sterne had known in Paris, shows the author frustrated with his subject: 'The duce take all sentiments! I wish there was not one in the world.' He continues, applying the imagery of childbirth to literary creation: 'I am going to ly-in; being at Christmas at my full reckoning—and unless what I shall bring forth is not *press'd* to death by these devils of printers, I shall have the honour of presenting to you a *couple of as clean brats* as ever chaste brain conceiv'd—they are frolicksome too.'[48] Sterne again promotes the cleanliness of his recent work – emerging from a 'chaste brain' the culmination of writing appears as a type of virgin birth (the volumes will even be ready by Christmas!). But there is a wryness about the imagery, and with his final remark Sterne hints (or perhaps he is tempting this particular correspondent) that there will be more to *A Sentimental Journey* than mere sentiment. In another letter – a flirtatious piece to an unidentified 'Hannah' – Sterne writes that his 'Journey ... shall make you cry as much as ever it made me laugh'.[49] Revealingly, he displays an ironic distance from sentiment, yet at the same time he is confident that sentimentally attuned readers will find satisfaction in his book. It is as though the work will serve different purposes for different readers (he believed *Tristram Shandy* offered several handles to readers, who variously would take 'the handle ... which suits their passions, their ignorance or sensibility').[50] *A Sentimental Journey* would provide pathos for those who sought it, while others might discover a more detached, self-conscious and ironic critique of the sentimentalism in which the work ostensibly participates.[51]

Volatility of this kind is evident throughout *A Sentimental Journey*. Scene after scene performs the work of sentimental literature, and with the immense flair and virtuosity of Sterne's style, it is easy to see why the work has been celebrated as a masterpiece of the genre. But repeatedly these scenes are also permeated with subtle counter-energies – irony, self-indulgence, carnality – which continually threaten to puncture the sentiment.[52] Staple features of sentimental heroism are selfless generosity and a desire to relieve distress; yet when Yorick performs acts of charity he is so conscious of his own benevolence that his motivation can seem self-serving. When he gives money to a group of beggars, he describes one who 'pull'd out a little handkerchief, and wiped his face as he turned away—and I thought he thank'd me more than them all' (pp. 36–7). His ultimate focus is upon his own place in the scene and upon his feelings, as later when he wipes the tears of the poor Maria: 'I felt such undescribable emotions within me . . . I am positive I have a soul' (p. 108). The 'official' purpose of such scenes in more straightforward sentimental writing is to invite readers to share in sympathy for the victim; Yorick draws the attention back to himself and the effect is of self-congratulation.

One early reader was reported to complain of *A Sentimental Journey* that 'when a man chooses to walk about the world with a cambrick handkerchief always in his hand, that he may always be ready to weep . . . he only turns me sick'.[53] Yorick's self-indulgence can indeed be seen as a flaw; but equally it might be recognized as part of an ironic exposure of a tension within sentimentalism – that self-interest is implicated in charity and sympathy. *A Sentimental Journey* participates in sentimentalism but not without drawing attention to its limitations. Similarly, Yorick's flirtations – coupled with the fact that he is at such pains to protest his carnal innocence – wittily probe the problematic borders between sensibility and sensuality. Sensibility, with its expression in blushes and tears, is inseparable from the body, yet sentimental bodies are often unreal, desexualized constructs. The hero of Mackenzie's *The Man of Feeling* can feel a young lady's heartbeat and hardly notice where his hand is; Yorick feels a lady's pulse at the wrist and the scene is charged with sexual tension. Ironically, though, Yorick's carnal interests become apparent only through the cumulative effect of his repeatedly denying them. When, for example, he wonders 'where would be the harm . . . if I was to beg of this distressed lady to accept of half of my chaise?—and what mighty mischief could ensue?' (pp. 22–3), his protracted contemplation hints at the considerable thought he has been giving to potential mischief. Collectively such expressions can unsettle the reliability of Yorick's supposedly candid account, but they remain assertions of innocent virtue nonetheless. Thus Sterne achieves a narrative which, for the most part, can be assimilated within chaste sentimental discourse, while inviting certain readers to enjoy a distinctly unsentimental mischief.

For Virginia Woolf, who introduced a 1928 World's Classics edition of *A Sentimental Journey*, Sterne's genius lay in his ability to capture lived experience – to convey in writing the fleeting moments of life and the erratic paths of sensation. With Sterne, she wrote, 'we are as close to life as we can be'.[54] She admired his delicate, flashing style, and praised Sterne's 'many passages of ... pure poetry',[55] which she exemplified with an extract from the Paris scenes:

I walked up gravely to the window in my dusty black coat, and looking through the glass saw all the world in yellow, blue, and green, running at the ring of pleasure.—The old with broken lances, and in helmets which had lost their vizards—the young in armour bright which shone like gold, beplumed with each gay feather of the east—all—all tilting at it like fascinated knights ... (p. 47)

Woolf is, of course, quite right that this is a striking and vivid passage, but interestingly she seems not to have picked up on other of its possible effects. In fact, in demonstrating Sterne's 'pure poetry', Woolf happened upon one of the book's most readily demonstrable passages of innuendo. 'Running at the ring' is a chivalric sport in which horsemen would attempt to lance a suspended metal hoop. Rabelais had exploited the sexual symbolism of the exercise in the bawdy *Gargantua and Pantagruel* (trans. 1653–94), from which Sterne borrowed the image firstly for *Tristram Shandy* ('They are running at the ring of pleasure, said I, giving him a prick').[56] He then re-used it in this passage, where the embedded innuendo is perhaps not obvious but, once noticed, can trigger a leakage of lewd meanings from the 'broken lances', the lost vizards, 'the young in armour' ('armour' was an eighteenth-century euphemism for a contraceptive) and the universal 'tilting' (a slang term for copulation). Such associations are clearly not what Woolf expected or wanted to find in good literature; that she didn't find them in *A Sentimental Journey* is very revealing of the subtle ambiguity Sterne was capable of creating.

Notes

1. To Lydia Sterne, 23 February 1767, *Letters of Laurence Sterne*, ed. Lewis Perry Curtis (Oxford: Clarendon Press, 1935), p. 301 (hereafter *Letters*).

2. To Thomas Becket, 3 September 1767, *Letters*, p. 393.

3. Details of Sterne's life and travels are derived from Arthur H. Cash's two-part biography, *Laurence Sterne: The Early and Middle Years* (London: Methuen, 1975) and *Laurence Sterne: The Later Years* (London: Methuen, 1986).

4. To an unidentified doctor, 30 January 1760, *Letters*, p. 90.

5. Laurence Sterne, *The Life and Opinions of Tristram Shandy, Gentleman*, ed. Melvyn New and Joan New (London: Penguin Books, 1997), p. 33 (hereafter *Tristram Shandy*).

6. Letter to Sir David Dalrymple, 4 April 1760, in *Sterne: The Critical Heritage*, ed. Alan B. Howes (London: Routledge & Kegan Paul, 1974), p. 55 (hereafter *Critical Heritage*).

7. *Tristram Shandy*, p. 54.

8. Ibid., p. 22.

9. Ibid., p. 24.

10. Letter to Thomas Gray, 8 March 1768, in *Critical Heritage*, p. 202.

11. *Critical Heritage*, pp. 204–8.

12. Owen Ruffhead, *Monthly Review*, no. 22 (May 1760), in *Critical Heritage*, p. 77.

13. To Mrs Daniel Draper, 12 April 1767, *Letters*, p. 322. *Letters* contains all of the extant parts of the '*Journal to Eliza*', first published in the *Works of Laurence Sterne*, ed. Wilbur L. Cross (New York: 1904).

14. Letter to the Reverend Weeden Butler, 19 March 1768, in *Critical Heritage*, pp. 202–3.

15. To John Hall-Stevenson, 12 August 1762, *Letters*, p. 180.

16. *Tristram Shandy*, p. 395.

17. Ibid., p. 396.

18. To Edward Stanley, 23 July 1766, *Letters*, p. 284.

19. For a dense, factual account of eighteenth-century travel, see Jeremy Black, *The British Abroad: The Grand Tour in the Eighteenth Century* (Stroud: Sutton, 1992). A stimulating collection of essays on eighteenth-century travel and imaginative literature is found in *All Before Them, English Literature and the Wider World, I: 1660–1780*, ed. John McVeagh (London: Ashfield Press, 1990).

20. To Robert Foley, 11 November 1764, *Letters*, p. 231.

21. *Tristram Shandy*, p. 398.

22. *Monthly Review*, no. 38 (April 1768), p. 314.

23. Tobias Smollett, *Travels through France and Italy*, ed. Frank Felsenstein (Oxford: Oxford University Press, 1981), p. 66.

24. See particularly John F. Sena, 'Smollett's Persona and the Melancholic Traveler: An Hypothesis', *Eighteenth-Century Studies*, 1 (1968), pp. 353–69; and R. D. Spector, 'Smollett's Traveler', in *Tobias Smollett: Bicentennial Essays Presented to Lewis M. Knapp*, ed. P.-G. Boucé and G. S. Rousseau (New York: Oxford University Press, 1971), pp. 231–46.

25. *Tristram Shandy*, p. 528.

26. Janet Todd's *Sensibility: An Introduction* (London and New York: Methuen, 1986) provides an accessible account of eighteenth-century 'sentiment' and its literary manifestations. My discussion is indebted to this work as well as other studies of the topic, particularly: G. J. Barker-Benfield, *The Culture of Sensibility: Sex and Society in Eighteenth-Century Britain* (Chicago: University of Chicago Press, 1992); R. F. Brissenden, *Virtue in Distress: Studies in the Novel of Sentiment from Richardson to Sade* (London: Macmillan, 1974); Markman Ellis, *The Politics of Sensibility: Race, Gender and Commerce in the Sentimental Novel* (Cambridge: Cambridge University Press, 1996); John Mullan, *Sentiment and Sociability: The Language of Feeling in the Eighteenth Century* (Oxford: Clarendon Press, 1988).

27. *The Correspondence of Samuel Richardson*, ed. Anna Laetitia Barbauld, 6 vols. (London: 1804), IV, pp. 282–3.

28. Quoted in Brissenden, *Virtue in Distress*, p. 106.

29. To John Wodehouse, 23 August 1765, *Letters*, p. 256.

30. James Boswell, *Life of Johnson*, ed. R. W. Chapman (Oxford: Oxford University Press, 1980), p. 480.

31. George Cheyne, *The English Malady*, ed. Roy Porter (London and New York: Routledge, 1991), p. 366.

32. Quoted in Ellis, *The Politics of Sensibility*, p. 35.

33. Quoted from *Eighteenth-Century Women Poets*, ed. Roger Lonsdale (Oxford: Oxford University Press, 1989), pp. 466–7 (the poem was published posthumously).

34. William Makepeace Thackeray, *The English Humourists of the Eighteenth Century* (London: Dent, 1949), p. 233.

35. Donald R. Wehrs, 'Levinas and Sterne: From the Ethics of the Face to the Aesthetics of Unrepresentability', in *Critical Essays on Laurence Sterne*, ed. Melvyn New (New York: G. K. Hall, 1998), pp. 311–29 (p. 311).

36. *Tristram Shandy*, p. 347.

37. *Critical Review*, no. 13 (January 1762), in *Critical Heritage*, p. 140.

38. *Monthly Review*, no. 26 (January 1762), in *Critical Heritage*, p. 141.

39. *Monthly Review*, no. 32 (February 1765), in *Critical Heritage*, pp. 167–8.

40. To Edward Stanley, 23 July 1766, *Letters*, p. 284.

41. *Tristram Shandy*, pp. 527–30.

42. To William Stanhope, 27 September 1767, *Letters*, pp. 395–6.

43. To Mrs William James, 12 November 1767, *Letters*, pp. 400–401.

44. To the Earl of —, 28 November 1767, *Letters*, pp. 402–3.

45. Richard Griffith, *A Series of Genuine Letters between Henry and Frances* (1770), quoted from *Critical Heritage*, p. 185.

46. *Monthly Review*, no. 32 (February 1765), in *Critical Heritage*, p. 167.

47. To Isaac Panchaud, 20 February 1767, *Letters*, p. 300.

48. To George Macartney, 3 December 1767, *Letters*, p. 405.

49. To Hannah, 15 November 1767, *Letters*, p. 401.

50. To Dr John Eustace, 9 February 1768, *Letters*, p. 411.

51. Mark Loveridge explores this tendency of the work in *Laurence Sterne and the Argument about Design* (London: Macmillan, 1982): 'What the reader makes of the book will depend, of course, on the nature of the reader. He can read one thing into it, or another: but basically the text of the *Journey* is neutral. It says one thing, and at the same time implies satire of it. But at bottom it is neither one thing nor the other. It is about the reader being forced to read, to make his choice' (p. 173).

52. For an early and influential reading of the work as a knowing, ironic critique of sentimentalism, see: Rufus Putney, 'The Evolution of *A Sentimental Journey*', *Philological Quarterly*, 19 (1940), pp. 349–69. Putney argues that the work was ultimately 'a hoax by which Sterne persuaded his contemporaries that the humor he wanted to write was the pathos they wished to read' (p. 368).

53. Frances Burney, *Memoirs of Doctor Burney* (1832), quoted from *Critical Heritage*, p. 204.

54. Laurence Sterne, *A Sentimental Journey through France and Italy*, introduction by Virginia Woolf (London: Oxford University Press, 1928), p. vii.

55. Ibid, p. xii.

56. *Tristram Shandy*, p. 444.

Further Reading

Editions

The best scholarly edition of *A Sentimental Journey* is that edited by Melvyn New and W. G. Day in volume VI of the Florida Edition of *The Works of Laurence Sterne* (Gainesville: University Press of Florida, 2002). This edition supplants (but does not altogether replace) the edition by Gardner D. Stout, Jr (Berkeley: University of California Press, 1967). For Sterne's *Sermons* and *The Life and Opinions of Tristram Shandy*, the Florida series provides the most comprehensively annotated and accurate texts. The Penguin Classics edition of *Tristram Shandy* (1997) is based on the Florida Edition and is recommended.

Letters of Laurence Sterne, ed. Lewis Perry Curtis (Oxford: Clarendon Press, 1935) is currently the best source for Sterne's correspondence and includes *The Journal to Eliza* (which, renamed *Continuation of the Bramine's Journal*, appears in volume VI of the Florida series together with *A Sentimental Journey*). Sterne's letters, including several discovered since Curtis's edition, will also be published as part of the Florida series.

Biography

Cash, Arthur H., *Laurence Sterne: The Early and Middle Years* (London: Methuen, 1975).
— *Laurence Sterne: The Later Years* (London: Methuen, 1986).
Ross, Ian Campbell, *Laurence Sterne: A Life* (Oxford: Oxford University Press, 2001).

Critical History and Reception

de Voogd, Peter and John Neubauer (eds.), *The Reception of Laurence Sterne in Europe* (London: Continuum, 2004).

Howes, Alan B., *Yorick and the Critics: Sterne's Reputation in England, 1760–1868* (New Haven: Yale University Press, 1958).

— ed., *Sterne: The Critical Heritage* (London: Routledge & Kegan Paul, 1974).

Works on Sterne and A Sentimental Journey

Battestin, Martin C., '*A Sentimental Journey* and the Syntax of Things', in *Augustan Worlds: Essays in Honour of A. R. Humphreys*, ed. J. C. Hilson, M. M. B. Jones and J. R. Watson (Leicester: Leicester University Press, 1978), pp. 223–9.

— 'Sterne Among the *Philosophes*: Body and Soul in *A Sentimental Journey*', *Eighteenth-Century Fiction* 7:1 (1994), pp. 17–36.

Berthoud, Jacques, 'The Beggar in *A Sentimental Journey*', *The Shandean* 3 (1991), pp. 37–48.

Brissenden, R. F., *Virtue in Distress: Studies in the Novel of Sentiment from Richardson to Sade* (London: Macmillan, 1974), part 2, chapter 3.

Chadwick, Joseph, 'Infinite Jest: Interpretation in Sterne's *A Sentimental Journey*', *Eighteenth-Century Studies* 12 (1978–9), pp. 190–205.

Descargues, Madeleine, '*A Sentimental Journey*, or "The Case of (In)delicacy"', in New (ed.), *Critical Essays*, pp. 243–53.

Donoghue, Frank, *The Fame Machine: Book Reviewing and Eighteenth-Century Literary Careers* (Stanford: Stanford University Press, 1996), chapter 2.

Dussinger, John A., 'Yorick and the "Eternal Fountain of our Feelings"', in *Psychology and Literature in the Eighteenth Century*, ed. Christopher Fox (New York: AMS Press, 1987), pp. 259–76.

Ellis, Markman, *The Politics of Sensibility: Race, Gender and Commerce in the Sentimental Novel* (Cambridge: Cambridge University Press, 1996), chapter 2.

Franssen, Paul, ' "Great Lessons of Political Instruction": The Earl of Clonmell Reads Sterne', *The Shandean* 2 (1990), pp. 152–201.

Harries, Elizabeth W., 'Sterne's Novels: Gathering Up the Fragments', *ELH* 49 (1982), pp. 35–49; (reprinted in New (ed.), *Critical Essays*, pp. 257–69).

Keymer, Tom, 'Marvell, Thomas Hollis, and Sterne's Maria: Parody in *A Sentimental Journey*', *The Shandean* 5 (1993), pp. 9–31.

Loveridge, Mark, *Laurence Sterne and the Argument About Design* (London: Macmillan, 1982), chapter 7.

Markley, Robert, 'Sentimentality as Performance: Shaftesbury, Sterne, and the Theatrics of Virtue', in *The New Eighteenth Century: Theory, Politics, English Literature*, ed. Felicity Nussbaum and Laura Brown (London: Methuen, 1987), pp. 210–30.

Mullan, John, *Sentiment and Sociability: The Language of Feeling in the Eighteenth Century* (Oxford: Clarendon Press, 1988), chapter 4.

— 'Sterne's Comedy of Sentiments', *Bulletin de la Société d'Études Anglo-Américaines des XVIIe et XVIIIe Siècles* 38 (1994), pp. 233–41.

New, Melvyn, 'Proust's Influence on Sterne: Remembrance of Things to Come', *Modern Language Notes* 103 (1988), pp. 1031–55; (reprinted in New (ed.), *Critical Essays*, pp. 177–97).

— ed., *Critical Essays on Laurence Sterne* (New York: G. K. Hall, 1998).

— 'Three Sentimental Journeys: Sterne, Shklovsky, Svevo', *The Shandean* 11 (1999–2000), pp. 126–34.

Seidel, Michael, 'Narrative Crossings: Sterne's *A Sentimental Journey*', *Genre* 18 (1985), pp. 1–22.

Tadié, Alexis, ' "Translating French Looks and Attitudes into Plain English": The Language of Gestures in Laurence Sterne's *A Sentimental Journey*', *Bulletin de la Société d'Études Anglo-Américaines des XVIIe et XVIIIe Siècles* 38 (1994), pp. 217–32.

Todd, Janet, *Sensibility: An Introduction* (London: Methuen, 1986), chapter 6.

Van Sant, Ann Jessie, *Eighteenth-Century Sensibility and the Novel: The Senses in Social Context* (Cambridge: Cambridge University Press, 1993), chapter 6.

Note on the Text

The first edition of *A Sentimental Journey* was published in two volumes by T. Becket and P. A. De Hondt in London on 27 February 1768. It appeared in two issues: a standard paper issue, and a large 'imperial' paper issue. The present edition is based on the large paper issue, and aims to reproduce as far as possible the often idiosyncratic nature of the original. For example, Sterne's extensive use of dashes of different lengths has been retained. Occasionally Sterne used different spellings for the same word and these variations have also been retained ('desart' and 'desert', for example, can be found in close proximity (p. 28)). Several eighteenth-century printing conventions have been altered: running quotation marks have been dropped; the long 's' has been modernized; spaces before punctuation marks have been closed. All footnotes are Sterne's; endnotes are my own.

Certain misprints have been silently corrected with reference to manuscript sources recorded in Gardner D. Stout's edition of the text (see Further Reading), and to Stout's record of slight differences between the large paper and standard paper issues. Sterne died on 18 March 1768, and there is no firm evidence that he revised the text for the second edition of 29 March 1768. The only occasions I have followed the second edition, therefore, are where I have removed superfluous accents that appear in the first: 'fille dè chambre' (p. 43); 'britheé' (p. 101). I have incorporated two additional emendations made in Ian Jack's edition (Oxford: Oxford University Press, 1968): 'ill off' for 'ill of' (p. 32); 'nor do I remember' for 'or do I remember' (p. 69). I have additionally emended: 'it's debtor' to 'its debtor' (p. 72) and 'louisd'ors' to 'louis d'ors' (p. 16).

A

SENTIMENTAL JOURNEY

THROUGH

FRANCE AND ITALY.

BY

Mr. YORICK.

VOL. I.

LONDON:

Printed for T. BECKET and P. A. DE HONDT,
in the Strand. MDCCLXVIII.

Advertisement[1]

THE Author begs leave to acknowledge to his Subscribers, that they have a further claim upon him for Two Volumes more than these delivered to them now, and which nothing but ill health could have prevented him, from having ready along with these.

The Work will be compleated and delivered to the Subscribers early the next Winter.

Asking us not to be passive readers

Space that you as reader occupy

A

SENTIMENTAL JOURNEY,

&c. &c.

THEY order, said I, this matter better in France—
—You have been in France? said my gentleman, turning quick upon me with the most civil triumph in the world.—Strange! quoth I, debating the matter with myself, That one and twenty miles sailing, for 'tis absolutely no further from Dover to Calais, should give a man these rights—I'll look into them: so giving up the argument—I went straight to my lodgings, put up half a dozen shirts and a black pair of silk breeches—"the coat I have on, said I, looking at the sleeve, will do"—took a place in the Dover stage; and the packet[2] sailing at nine the next morning—by three I had got sat down to my dinner upon a fricassee'd chicken so incontestably in France, that had I died that night of an indigestion, the whole world could not have suspended the effects of the *Droits d'aubaine*[3]—my shirts, and black pair of silk breeches—portmanteau and all must have gone to the King of France—even the little picture which I have so long worn, and so often have told thee, Eliza,[4] I would carry with me into my grave, would have been torn from my neck.—Ungenerous!—to seize upon the wreck of an unwary passenger, whom your subjects had beckon'd to their coast—by heaven! SIRE, it is not well done; and much does it grieve me, 'tis the monarch of a people so civilized and courteous, and so renown'd for sentiment and fine feelings, that I have to reason with——

But I have scarce set foot in your dominions——

---

* All the effects of strangers (Swiss and Scotch excepted) dying in France, are seized by virtue of this law, tho' the heir be upon the spot —— the profit of these contingencies being farm'd, there is no redress.

CALAIS.

WHEN I had finish'd my dinner, and drank the King of France's health, to satisfy my mind that I bore him no spleen, but, on the contrary, high honour for the humanity of his temper—I rose up an inch taller for the accommodation.

—No—said I—the Bourbon is by no means a cruel race: they may be misled like other people; but there is a mildness in their blood. As I acknowledged this, I felt a suffusion of a finer kind upon my cheek— more warm and friendly to man, than what Burgundy (at least of two livres a bottle, which was such as I had been drinking) could have produced.

—Just God! said I, kicking my portmanteau aside, what is there in this world's goods which should sharpen our spirits, and make so many kind-hearted brethren of us, fall out so cruelly as we do by the way?

When man is at peace with man, how much lighter than a feather is the heaviest of metals in his hand! he pulls out his purse, and holding it airily and uncompress'd, looks round him, as if he sought for an object to share it with—In doing this, I felt every vessel in my frame dilate—the arteries beat all chearily together, and every power which sustained life, perform'd it with so little friction, that 'twould have confounded the most *physical precieuse* in France: with all her materialism, she could scarce have called me a machine—[5]

I'm confident, said I to myself, I should have overset her creed.

The accession of that idea, carried nature, at that time, as high as she could go—I was at peace with the world before, and this finish'd the treaty with myself—

—Now, was I a King of France, cried I—what a moment for an orphan to have begg'd his father's portmanteau of me!

[handwritten margin notes: Doctrine from Enlightenment · no pre-existing soul · everybody is like a machine / God put motion into these machines]

THE MONK.
CALAIS.

I HAD scarce utter'd the words, when a poor monk of the order of St. Francis came into the room to beg something for his convent. No man cares to have his virtues the sport of contingencies—or one man may be generous, as another man is puissant—*sed non, quo ad hanc*[6]—or be it as it may—for there is no regular reasoning upon the ebbs and flows of our humours; they may depend upon the same causes, for ought I know, which influence the tides themselves—'twould oft be no discredit to us, to suppose it was so: I'm sure at least for myself, that in many a case I should be more highly satisfied, to have it said by the world, "I had had an affair with the moon, in which there was neither sin nor shame," than have it pass altogether as my own act and deed, wherein there was so much of both.

—But be this as it may. The moment I cast my eyes upon him, I was predetermined not to give him a single sous; and accordingly I put my purse into my pocket—button'd it up—set myself a little more upon my centre, and advanced up gravely to him: there was something, I fear, forbidding in my look: I have his figure this moment before my eyes, and think there was that in it which deserved better.

The monk, as I judged from the break in his tonsure, a few scatter'd white hairs upon his temples, being all that remained of it, might be about seventy—but from his eyes, and that sort of fire which was in them, which seemed more temper'd by courtesy than years, could be no more than sixty—Truth might lie between—He was certainly sixty-five; and the general air of his countenance, notwithstanding something seem'd to have been planting wrinkles in it before their time, agreed to the account.

It was one of those heads, which Guido[7] has often painted—mild, pale—penetrating, free from all common-place ideas of fat contented ignorance looking downwards upon the earth—it look'd forwards; but look'd, as if it look'd at something beyond this world. How one of his order came by it, heaven above, who let it fall upon a monk's shoulders, best knows: but it would have suited a Bramin,[8] and had I met it upon the plains of Indostan, I had reverenced it.

The rest of his outline may be given in a few strokes; one might put it into the hands of any one to design, for 'twas neither elegant or otherwise, but as character and expression made it so: it was a thin, spare form, something above the common size, if it lost not the distinction by a bend forwards in the figure—but it was the attitude of Intreaty; and as it now stands presented to my imagination, it gain'd more than it lost by it.

When he had enter'd the room three paces, he stood still; and laying his left hand upon his breast, (a slender white staff with which he journey'd being in his right)—when I had got close up to him, he introduced himself with the little story of the wants of his convent, and the poverty of his order—and did it with so simple a grace—and such an air of deprecation was there in the whole cast of his look and figure—I was bewitch'd not to have been struck with it—

—A better reason was, I had predetermined not to give him a single sous.

THE MONK.
CALAIS.

'TIS very true, said I, replying to a cast upwards with his eyes, — with which he had concluded his address—'tis very true— and heaven be their resource who have no other but the charity of the world, the stock of which, I fear, is no way sufficient for the many *great claims* which are hourly made upon it.

As I pronounced the words *great claims*, he gave a slight glance with his eye downwards upon the sleeve of his tunick—I felt the full force of the appeal—I acknowledge it, said I—a coarse habit, and that but once in three years, with meagre diet—are no great matters; and the true point of pity is, as they can be earn'd in the world with so little industry, that your order should wish to procure them by pressing upon a fund which is the property of the lame, the blind, the aged and the infirm—the captive who lies down counting over and over again the days of his afflictions, languishes also for his share of it; and had you been of the *order of mercy*, instead of the order of St. Francis,[9] poor as I am, continued I, pointing at my portmanteau, full chearfully should it have been open'd to you, for the ransom of the unfortunate—The monk made me a bow—but of all others, resumed I, the unfortunate of our own country, surely, have the first rights; and I have left thousands in distress upon our own shore—The monk gave a cordial wave with his head—as much as to say, No doubt, there is misery enough in every corner of the world, as well as within our convent— But we distinguish, said I, laying my hand upon the sleeve of his tunick, in return for his appeal—we distinguish, my good Father! betwixt those who wish only to eat the bread of their own labour—and those who eat the bread of other people's, and have no other plan in life, but to get through it in sloth and ignorance, *for the love of God*.[10]

The poor Franciscan made no reply: a hectic of a moment[11] pass'd across his cheek, but could not tarry—Nature seemed to have had done with her resentments in him; he shewed none—but letting his staff fall within his arm, he press'd both his hands with resignation upon his breast, and retired.

THE MONK.
CALAIS.

M Y heart smote me the moment he shut the door—Psha! said I with an air of carelessness, three several times—but it would not do: every ungracious syllable I had utter'd, crouded back into my imagination: I reflected, I had no right over the poor Franciscan, but to deny him; and that the punishment of that was enough to the disappointed without the addition of unkind language—I consider'd his grey hairs—his courteous figure seem'd to re-enter and gently ask me what injury he had done me?—and why I could use him thus—I would have given twenty livres for an advocate—I have behaved very ill; said I within myself; but I have only just set out upon my travels; and shall learn better manners as I get along.

THE DESOBLIGEANT.
CALAIS.

WHEN a man is discontented with himself, it has one advantage however, that it puts him into an excellent frame of mind for making a bargain. Now there being no travelling through France and Italy without a chaise—and nature generally prompting us to the thing we are fittest for, I walk'd out into the coach yard to buy or hire something of that kind to my purpose: an old * Desobligeant in the furthest corner of the court, hit my fancy at first sight, so I instantly got into it, and finding it in tolerable harmony with my feelings, I ordered the waiter to call Monsieur Dessein[12] the master of the hôtel— but Monsieur Dessein being gone to vespers, and not caring to face the Franciscan whom I saw on the opposite side of the court, in conference with a lady just arrived, at the inn—I drew the taffeta curtain betwixt us, and being determined to write my journey, I took out my pen and ink, and wrote the preface to it in the *Desobligeant.*

* A chaise, so called in France, from its holding but one person.

PREFACE
IN THE DESOBLIGEANT.

teaching within

I T must have been observed by many a peripatetic philosopher,[13] That nature has set up by her own unquestionable authority certain boundaries and fences to circumscribe the discontent of man: she has effected her purpose in the quietest and easiest manner by laying him under almost insuperable obligations to work out his ease, and to sustain his sufferings at home. It is there only that she has provided him with the most suitable objects to partake of his happiness, and bear a part of that burden which in all countries and ages, has ever been too heavy for one pair of shoulders. 'Tis true we are endued with an imperfect power of spreading our happiness sometimes beyond *her* limits, but 'tis so ordered, that from the want of languages, connections, and dependencies, and from the difference in education, customs and habits, we lie under so many impediments in communicating our sensations out of our own sphere, as often amount to a total impossibility.

It will always follow from hence, that the balance of sentimental commerce is always against the expatriated adventurer: he must buy what he has little occasion for at their own price—his conversation will seldom be taken in exchange for theirs without a large discount— and this, by the by, eternally driving him into the hands of more equitable brokers for such conversation as he can find, it requires no great spirit of divination to guess at his party—

This brings me to my point; and naturally leads me (if the see-saw of this *Desobligeant* will but let me get on) into the efficient as well as the final causes[14] of travelling—

Your idle people that leave their native country and go abroad for some reason or reasons which may be derived from one of these general causes—

> Infirmity of body,
> Imbecility of mind, or
> Inevitable necessity.

The first two include all those who travel by land or by water, labouring with pride, curiosity, vanity or spleen, subdivided and combined *in infinitum*.

The third class includes the whole army of peregrine martyrs; more especially those travellers who set out upon their travels with the benefit of the clergy,[15] either as delinquents travelling under the direction of governors recommended by the magistrate—or young gentlemen transported by the cruelty of parents and guardians, and travelling under the direction of governors recommended by Oxford, Aberdeen and Glasgow.

There is a fourth class, but their number is so small that they would not deserve a distinction, was it not necessary in a work of this nature to observe the greatest precision and nicety, to avoid a confusion of character. And these men I speak of, are such as cross the seas and sojourn in a land of strangers with a view of saving money for various reasons and upon various pretences: but as they might also save themselves and others a great deal of unnecessary trouble by saving their money at home—and as their reasons for travelling are the least complex of any other species of emigrants, I shall distinguish these gentlemen by the name of

> Simple Travellers.

Thus the whole circle of travellers may be reduced to the following *Heads*.

> Idle Travellers,
> Inquisitive Travellers,
> Lying Travellers,
> Proud Travellers,
> Vain Travellers,
> Splenetic Travellers.

Then follow the Travellers of Necessity.

The delinquent and felonious Traveller,

The unfortunate and innocent Traveller,

The simple Traveller,

And last of all (if you please) The

Sentimental Traveller (meaning thereby myself) who have travell'd, and of which I am now sitting down to give an account—as much out of *Necessity*, and the *besoin de* Voyager,[16] as any one in the class.

[handwritten margin note: always awareness brought to him writing this out.]

I am well aware, at the same time, as both my travels and observations will be altogether of a different cast from any of my fore-runners; that I might have insisted upon a whole nitch entirely to myself—but I should break in upon the confines of the *Vain* Traveller, in wishing to draw attention towards me, till I have some better grounds for it, than the mere *Novelty of my Vehicle.*

It is sufficient for my reader, if he has been a traveller himself, that with study and reflection hereupon he may be able to determine his own place and rank in the catalogue—it will be one step towards knowing himself; as it is great odds, but he retains some tincture and resemblance, of what he imbibed or carried out, to the present hour.

The man who first transplanted the grape of Burgundy to the Cape of Good Hope (observe he was a Dutch man) never dreamt of drinking the same wine at the Cape, that the same grape produced upon the French mountains—he was too phlegmatic for that—but undoubtedly he expected to drink some sort of vinous liquor; but whether good, bad, or indifferent—he knew enough of this world to know, that it did not depend upon his choice, but that what is generally called *chance* was to decide his success: however, he hoped for the best; and in these hopes, by an intemperate confidence in the fortitude of his head, and the depth of his discretion, *Mynheer*[17] might possibly overset both in his new vineyard; and by discovering his nakedness,[18] become a laughing-stock to his people.

Even so it fares with the poor Traveller, sailing and posting through the politer kingdoms of the globe in pursuit of knowledge and improvements.

Knowledge and improvements are to be got by sailing and posting for that purpose; but whether useful knowledge and real improvements, is all a lottery—and even where the adventurer is successful, the acquired stock must be used with caution and sobriety to turn to any profit—but as the chances run prodigiously the other way both as to the acquisition and application, I am of opinion, That a man would act as wisely, if he could prevail upon himself, to live contented without foreign knowledge or foreign improvements, especially if he lives in a country that has no absolute want of either—and indeed, much grief of heart has it oft and many a time cost me, when I have observed how many a foul step the inquisitive Traveller has measured to see sights and look into discoveries; all which, as Sancho Pança said to Don Quixote, they might have seen dry-shod at home.[19] It is an age so full of light, that there is scarce a country or corner of Europe whose beams are not crossed and interchanged with others—Knowledge in most of its branches, and in most affairs, is like music in an Italian street, whereof those may partake, who pay nothing—But there is no nation under heaven—and God is my record, (before whose tribunal I must one day come and give an account of this work)—that I do not speak it vauntingly—But there is no nation under heaven abounding with more variety of learning—where the sciences may be more fitly woo'd, or more surely won than here—where art is encouraged, and will so soon rise high—where Nature (take her all together) has so little to answer for—and, to close all, where there is more wit and variety of character to feed the mind with—Where then, my dear countrymen, are you going—[20]

—We are only looking at this chaise, said they—Your most obedient servant, said I, skipping out of it, and pulling off my hat—We were wondering, said one of them, who, I found, was an *inquisitive traveller*— what could occasion its motion.——'Twas the agitation, said I coolly, of writing a preface—I never heard, said the other, who was a *simple traveller*, of a preface wrote in a *Desobligeant*.—It would have been better, said I, in a *Vis a Vis*.[21]

—*As an English man does not travel to see English men*, I retired to my room.

CALAIS.

I PERCEIVED that something darken'd the passage more than myself, as I stepp'd along it to my room; it was effectually[22] Mons. Dessein, the master of the hôtel, who had just return'd from vespers, and, with his hat under his arm, was most complaisantly following me, to put me in mind of my wants. I had wrote myself pretty well out of conceit with the *Desobligeant*; and Mons. Dessein speaking of it, with a shrug, as if it would no way suit me, it immediately struck my fancy that it belong'd to some *innocent traveller*, who, on his return home, had left it to Mons. Dessein's honour to make the most of. Four months had elapsed since it had finish'd its career of Europe in the corner of Mons. Dessein's coach-yard; and having sallied out from thence but a vampt-up business at the first, though it had been twice taken to pieces on Mount Sennis,[23] it had not profited much by its adventures—but by none so little as the standing so many months unpitied in the corner of Mons. Dessein's coach-yard. Much indeed was not to be said for it—but something might—and when a few words will rescue misery out of her distress, I hate the man who can be a churl of them.

—Now was I the master of this hôtel, said I, laying the point of my fore-finger on Mons. Dessein's breast, I would inevitably make a point of getting rid of this unfortunate *Desobligeant*—it stands swinging reproaches at you every time you pass by it—

Mon Dieu![24] said Mons. Dessein—I have no interest—Except the interest, said I, which men of a certain turn of mind take, Mons. Dessein, in their own sensations—I'm persuaded, to a man who feels for others as well as for himself, every rainy night, disguise it as you will, must cast a damp upon your spirits—You suffer, Mons. Dessein, as much as the machine—

I have always observed, when there is as much *sour* as *sweet* in a compliment, that an Englishman is eternally at a loss within himself, whether to take it, or let it alone: a Frenchman never is: Mons. Dessein made me a bow.

C'est bien vrai,[25] said he—But in this case I should only exchange one disquietude for another, and with loss: figure to yourself, my dear Sir, that in giving you a chaise which would fall to pieces before you had got half way to Paris—figure to yourself how much I should suffer, in giving an ill impression of myself to a man of honour, and lying at the mercy, as I must do, *d'un homme d'esprit*.[26]

The dose was made up exactly after my own prescription; so I could not help taking it—and returning Mons. Dessein his bow, without more casuistry we walk'd together towards his Remise,[27] to take a view of his magazine of chaises.

IN THE STREET.
CALAIS.

IT must needs be a hostile kind of a world, when the buyer (if it be but of a sorry post-chaise) cannot go forth with the seller thereof into the street to terminate the difference betwixt them, but he instantly falls into the same frame of mind and views his conventionist[28] with the same sort of eye, as if he was going along with him to Hyde-park corner to fight a duel.[29] For my own part, being but a poor sword's-man, and no way a match for Monsieur *Dessein*, I felt the rotation of all the movements within me, to which the situation is incident—I looked at Monsieur *Dessein* through and through—ey'd him as he walked along in profile— then, *en face*[30]—thought he look'd like a Jew—then a Turk[31]—disliked his wig—cursed him by my gods—wished him at the devil—

—And is all this to be lighted up in the heart for a beggarly account of three or four louis d'ors,[32] which is the most I can be overreach'd in?—Base passion! said I, turning myself about, as a man naturally does upon a sudden reverse of sentiment—base, ungentle passion! thy hand is against every man, and every man's hand against thee[33]—heaven forbid! said she, raising her hand up to her forehead, for I had turned full in front upon the lady whom I had seen in conference with the monk—she had followed us unperceived—Heaven forbid indeed! said

I, offering her my own—she had a black pair of silk gloves open only at the thumb and two fore-fingers, so accepted it without reserve—and I led her up to the door of the Remise.

Monsieur *Dessein* had *diabled*[34] the key above fifty times before he found out he had come with a wrong one in his hand: we were as impatient as himself to have it open'd; and so attentive to the obstacle, that I continued holding her hand almost without knowing it; so that Monsieur *Dessein* left us together with her hand in mine, and with our faces turned towards the door of the Remise, and said he would be back in five minutes.

Now a colloquy of five minutes, in such a situation, is worth one of as many ages, with your faces turned towards the street: in the latter case, 'tis drawn from the objects and occurrences without—when your eyes are fixed upon a dead blank—you draw purely from yourselves. A silence of a single moment upon Monsieur *Dessein*'s leaving us, had been fatal to the situation—she had infallibly turned about—so I begun the conversation instantly.—

—But what were the temptations, (as I write not to apologize for the weaknesses of my heart in this tour,—but to give an account of them)—shall be described with the same simplicity, with which I felt them.

THE REMISE DOOR.
CALAIS.

WHEN I told the reader that I did not care to get out of the *Desobligeant*, because I saw the monk in close conference with a lady just arrived at the inn—I told him the truth; but I did not tell him the whole truth;[35] for I was full as much restrained by the appearance and figure of the lady he was talking to. Suspicion crossed my brain, and said, he was telling her what had passed: something jarred upon it within me—I wished him at his convent.

When the heart flies out before the understanding, it saves the judgment a world of pains—I was certain she was of a better order of beings—however, I thought no more of her, but went on and wrote my preface.

The impression returned, upon my encounter with her in the street; a guarded frankness with which she gave me her hand, shewed, I thought, her good education and her good sense; and as I led her on, I felt a pleasurable ductility about her, which spread a calmness over all my spirits—

—Good God! how a man might lead such a creature as this round the world with him!— → *inner thoughts*

I had not yet seen her face—'twas not material; for the drawing was instantly set about, and long before we had got to the door of the Remise, *Fancy* had finished the whole head, and pleased herself as much with its fitting her goddess, as if she had dived into the TIBER for it[36]—but thou art a seduced, and a seducing slut; and albeit thou cheatest us seven times a day with thy pictures and images, yet with so many charms dost thou do it, and thou deckest out thy pictures in the shapes of so many angels of light, 'tis a shame to break with thee.

When we had got to the door of the Remise, she withdrew her hand from across her forehead, and let me see the original—it was a face of about six and twenty—of a clear transparent brown, simply set off without rouge or powder—it was not critically handsome, but there was that in it, which in the frame of mind I was in, which attached me much more to it—it was interesting; I fancied it wore the characters of a widow'd look, and in that state of its declension, which had passed the two first paroxysms of sorrow, and was quietly beginning to reconcile itself to its loss—but a thousand other distresses might have traced the same lines; I wish'd to know what they had been—and was ready to enquire, (had the same *bon ton*[37] of conversation permitted, as in the days of Esdras)—"*What aileth thee? and why art thou disquieted? and why is thy understanding troubled?*"—In a word, I felt benevolence for her; and resolved some way or other to throw in my mite of courtesy[38]—if not of service.

Such were my temptations—and in this disposition to give way to them, was I left alone with the lady with her hand in mine, and with

allusion to religion

our faces both turned closer to the door of the Remise than what was absolutely necessary.

THE REMISE DOOR.
CALAIS.

THIS certainly, fair lady! said I, raising her hand up a little lightly as I began, must be one of Fortune's whimsical doings: to take two utter strangers by their hands—of different sexes, and perhaps from different corners of the globe, and in one moment place them together in such a cordial situation, as Friendship herself could scarce have atchieved for them, had she projected it for a month—

—And your reflection upon it, shews how much, Monsieur, she has embarassed you by the adventure.—

When the situation is, what we would wish, nothing is so ill-timed as to hint at the circumstances which make it so: you thank Fortune, continued she—you had reason—the heart knew it, and was satisfied; and who but an English philosopher would have sent notices of it to the brain to reverse the judgment?

In saying this, she disengaged her hand with a look which I thought a sufficient commentary upon the text.

It is a miserable picture which I am going to give of the weakness of my heart, by owning, that it suffered a pain, which worthier occasions could not have inflicted.—I was mortified with the loss of her hand, and the manner in which I had lost it carried neither oil nor wine to the wound:[39] I never felt the pain of a sheepish inferiority so miserably in my life.

The triumphs of a true feminine heart are short upon these discomfitures. In a very few seconds she laid her hand upon the cuff of my coat, in order to finish her reply; so some way or other, God knows how, I regained my situation.

—She had nothing to add.

I forthwith began to model a different conversation for the lady, thinking from the spirit as well as moral of this, that I had been mistaken in her character; but upon turning her face towards me, the spirit which had animated the reply was fled—the muscles relaxed, and I beheld the same unprotected look of distress which first won me to her interest—melancholy! to see such sprightliness the prey of sorrow.— I pitied her from my soul; and though it may seem ridiculous enough to a torpid heart,—I could have taken her into my arms, and cherished her, though it was in the open street, without blushing.

The pulsations of the arteries along my fingers pressing across hers, told her what was passing within me: she looked down—a silence of some moments followed.

I fear, in this interval, I must have made some slight efforts towards a closer compression of her hand, from a subtle sensation I felt in the palm of my own—not as if she was going to withdraw hers—but, as if she thought about it—and I had infallibly lost it a second time, had not instinct more than reason directed me to the last resource in these dangers—to hold it loosely, and in a manner as if I was every moment going to release it, of myself; so she let it continue, till Monsieur *Dessein* returned with the key; and in the mean time I set myself to consider how I should undo the ill impressions which the poor monk's story, in case he had told it her, must have planted in her breast against me.

THE SNUFF-BOX.
CALAIS.

THE good old monk was within six paces of us, as the idea of him cross'd my mind; and was advancing towards us a little out of the line, as if uncertain whether he should break in upon us or no.— He stopp'd, however, as soon as he came up to us, with a world of frankness; and having a horn snuff-box in his hand, he presented it open to me—You shall taste mine—said I, pulling out my box (which was a small tortoise one) and putting it into his hand—'Tis most excellent, said the monk; Then do me the favour, I replied, to accept of the box and all, and when you take a pinch out of it, sometimes recollect it was the peace-offering of a man who once used you unkindly, but not from his heart.

The poor monk blush'd as red as scarlet. *Mon Dieu!* said he, pressing his hands together—you never used me unkindly.—I should think, said the lady, he is not likely. I blush'd in my turn; but from what movements, I leave to the few who feel to analyse—Excuse me, Madame, replied I—I treated him most unkindly; and from no provocations—'Tis impossible, said the lady.—My God! cried the monk, with a warmth of asseveration which seemed not to belong to him— the fault was in me, and in the indiscretion of my zeal—the lady opposed it, and I joined with her in maintaining it was impossible, that a spirit so regulated as his, could give offence to any.

I knew not that contention could be rendered so sweet and pleasurable a thing to the nerves as I then felt it.—We remained silent, without any sensation of that foolish pain which takes place, when in such a circle you look for ten minutes in one another's faces without saying a word. Whilst this lasted, the monk rubb'd his horn box upon the sleeve of his tunick; and as soon as it had acquired a little air of brightness by the friction—he made a low bow, and said, 'twas too late to say whether it was the weakness or goodness of our tempers which had involved us in this contest—but be it as it would—he begg'd we might exchange boxes—In saying this, he presented his to me with one hand, as he took mine from me in the other; and having kiss'd it—with a stream of good nature in his eyes he put it into his bosom—and took his leave.

I guard this box, as I would the instrumental parts of my religion, to help my mind on to something better: in truth, I seldom go abroad without it; and oft and many a time have I called up by it the courteous spirit of its owner to regulate my own, in the justlings of the world; they had found full employment for his, as I learnt from his story, till about the forty-fifth year of his age, when upon some military services ill requited, and meeting at the same time with a disappointment in the tenderest of passions, he abandon'd the sword and the sex together, and took sanctuary, not so much in his convent as in himself.

I feel a damp upon my spirits, as I am going to add, that in my last return through Calais, upon inquiring after Father Lorenzo, I heard he had been dead near three months, and was buried, not in his convent, but, according to his desire, in a little cimetiery belonging to it, about two leagues off: I had a strong desire to see where they had laid him—when, upon pulling out his little horn box, as I sat by his grave, and plucking up a nettle or two at the head of it, which had no business to grow there, they all struck together so forcibly upon my affections, that I burst into a flood of tears—but I am as weak as a woman; and I beg the world not to smile, but pity me.

THE REMISE DOOR.
CALAIS.

I HAD never quitted the lady's hand all this time; and had held it so long, that it would have been indecent to have let it go, without first pressing it to my lips: the blood and spirits, which had suffer'd a revulsion from her, crouded back to her, as I did it.

Now the two travellers who had spoke to me in the coach-yard, happening at that crisis to be passing by, and observing our communications, naturally took it into their heads that we must be *man and wife* at least; so stopping as soon as they came up to the door of the Remise, the one of them, who was the inquisitive traveller, ask'd us, if we set out for Paris the next morning?—I could only answer for myself, I said; and the lady added, she was for Amiens.—We dined there yesterday, said the simple traveller—You go directly through the town, added the other, in your road to Paris. I was going to return a thousand thanks for the intelligence, *that Amiens was in the road to Paris*; but, upon pulling out my poor monk's little horn box to take a pinch of snuff—I made them a quiet bow, and wishing them a good passage to Dover—they left us alone—

—Now where would be the harm, said I to myself, if I was to beg of this distressed lady to accept of half of my chaise?—and what mighty mischief could ensue?

Every dirty passion, and bad propensity in my nature, took the alarm, as I stated the proposition—It will oblige you to have a third horse, said AVARICE, which will put twenty livres out of your pocket.— You know not who she is, said CAUTION—or what scrapes the affair may draw you into, whisper'd COWARDICE—

Depend upon it, Yorick! said DISCRETION, 'twill be said you went off with a mistress, and came by assignation to Calais for that purpose—

—You can never after, cried HYPOCRISY aloud, shew your face in the world—or rise, quoth MEANNESS, in the church—or be any thing in it, said PRIDE, but a lousy prebendary.

—But 'tis a civil thing, said I—and as I generally act from the first impulse, and therefore seldom listen to these cabals, which serve no purpose, that I know of, but to encompass the heart with adamant—I turn'd instantly about to the lady—

—But she had glided off unperceived, as the cause was pleading, and had made ten or a dozen paces down the street, by the time I had made the determination; so I set off after her with a long stride, to make her the proposal with the best address I was master of; but observing she walk'd with her cheek half resting upon the palm of her hand—with the slow, short-measur'd step of thoughtfulness, and with her eyes, as she went step by step, fix'd upon the ground, it struck me, she was trying the same cause herself.—God help her! said I, she has some mother-in-law, or tartufish[40] aunt, or nonsensical old woman, to consult upon the occasion, as well as myself: so not caring to interrupt the processe, and deeming it more gallant to take her at discretion than by surprize, I faced about, and took a short turn or two before the door of the Remise, whilst she walk'd musing on one side.

IN THE STREET.
CALAIS.

HAVING, on first sight of the lady, settled the affair in my fancy, "that she was of the better order of beings"—and then laid it down as a second axiom, as indisputable as the first, That she was a widow, and wore a character of distress—I went no further; I got ground enough for the situation which pleased me—and had she remained close beside my elbow till midnight, I should have held true to my system, and considered her only under that general idea.

She had scarce got twenty paces distant from me, ere something within me called out for a more particular inquiry—it brought on the idea of a further separation—I might possibly never see her more— the heart is for saving what it can; and I wanted the traces thro' which my wishes might find their way to her, in case I should never rejoin her myself: in a word, I wish'd to know her name—her family's—her condition; and as I knew the place to which she was going, I wanted to know from whence she came: but there was no coming at all this intelligence: a hundred little delicacies stood in the way. I form'd a score different plans—There was no such thing as a man's asking her directly—the thing was impossible.

A little French *debonaire* captain, who came dancing down the street, shewed me, it was the easiest thing in the world; for popping in betwixt us, just as the lady was returning back to the door of the Remise, he introduced himself to my acquaintance, and before he had well got announced, begg'd I would do him the honour to present him to the lady—I had not been presented myself—so turning about to her, he did it just as well by asking her, if she had come from Paris?—No: she was going that rout, she said.—*Vous n'etez pas de Londre?*—She was not, she replied.—Then Madame must have come thro' Flanders.— *Apparamment vous etez Flammande?* said the French captain.—The lady answered, she was.—*Peutetre, de Lisle?*[41] added he—She said, she was not of Lisle.—Nor Arras?—nor Cambray?—nor Ghent?—nor Brussels? She answered, she was of Brussels.

He had had the honour, he said, to be at the bombardment of it last war—that it was finely situated, *pour cela*—and full of noblesse when the Imperialists were driven out by the French[42] (the lady made a slight curtsy)—so giving her an account of the affair, and of the share he had had in it—he begg'd the honour to know her name—so made his bow.

—*Et Madame a son Mari?*[43]—said he, looking back when he had made two steps—and without staying for an answer—danced down the street.

Had I served seven years apprenticeship to good breeding, I could not have done as much.

THE REMISE.
CALAIS.

AS the little French captain left us, Mons. Dessein came up with the key of the Remise in his hand, and forthwith let us into his magazine of chaises.

The first object which caught my eye, as Mons. Dessein open'd the door of the Remise, was another old tatter'd *Desobligeant:* and notwithstanding it was the exact picture of that which had hit my fancy so much in the coach-yard but an hour before—the very sight of it stirr'd up a disagreeable sensation within me now; and I thought 'twas a churlish beast into whose heart the idea could first enter, to construct such a machine; nor had I much more charity for the man who could think of using it.

I observed the lady was as little taken with it as myself: so Mons. Dessein led us on to a couple of chaises which stood abreast, telling us as he recommended them, that they had been purchased by my Lord A. and B. to go the *grand tour*, but had gone no further than Paris, so were in all respects as good as new—They were too good—so I pass'd on to a third, which stood behind, and forthwith began to chaffer[44] for the price—But 'twill scarce hold two, said I, opening the door and getting in—Have the goodness, Madam, said Mons. Dessein, offering his arm, to step in—The lady hesitated half a second, and stepp'd in; and the waiter that moment beckoning to speak to Mons. Dessein, he shut the door of the chaise upon us, and left us.

THE REMISE.
CALAIS.

C'EST bien comique,[45] 'tis very droll, said the lady smiling, from the reflection that this was the second time we had been left together by a parcel of nonsensical contingencies—*c'est bien comique,* said she—

—There wants nothing, said I, to make it so, but the comick use which the gallantry of a Frenchman would put it to—to make love the first moment, and an offer of his person the second.

'Tis their *fort.*[46] replied the lady.

It is supposed so at least—and how it has come to pass, continued I, I know not; but they have certainly got the credit of understanding more of love, and making it better than any other nation upon earth: but for my own part I think them errant bunglers, and in truth the worst set of marksmen that ever tried Cupid's patience.

—To think of making love by *sentiments!*

I should as soon think of making a genteel suit of cloaths out of remnants:—and to do it—pop—at first sight by declaration—is submitting the offer and themselves with it, to be sifted, with all their *pours* and *contres,*[47] by an unheated mind.

The lady attended as if she expected I should go on.

Consider then, madam, continued I, laying my hand upon hers—

That grave people hate Love for the name's sake—

That selfish people hate it for their own—

Hypocrites for heaven's—

And that all of us both old and young, being ten times worse frighten'd than hurt by the very *report*—What a want of knowledge in this branch of commerce a man betrays, whoever lets the word come out of his lips, till an hour or two at least after the time, that his silence upon it becomes tormenting. A course of small, quiet attentions, not so pointed as to alarm—nor so vague as to be misunderstood,—with now and then a look of kindness, and little or nothing said upon it—leaves Nature for your mistress, and she fashions it to her mind.—

Then I solemnly declare, said the lady, blushing—you have been making love to me all this while.

THE REMISE.
CALAIS.

MONSIEUR *Dessein* came back to let us out of the chaise, and acquaint the lady, the Count de L———— her brother was just arrived at the hotel. Though I had infinite good will for the lady, I cannot say, that I rejoiced in my heart at the event—and could not help telling her so—for it is fatal to a proposal, Madam, said I, that I was going to make you—

—You need not tell me what the proposal was, said she, laying her hand upon both mine, as she interrupted me.—A man, my good Sir, has seldom an offer of kindness to make to a woman, but she has a presentiment of it some moments before—

Nature arms her with it, said I, for immediate preservation—But I think, said she, looking in my face, I had no evil to apprehend—and to deal frankly with you, had determined to accept it.—If I had—(she stopped a moment)—I believe your good will would have drawn a story from me, which would have made pity the only dangerous thing in the journey.

In saying this, she suffered me to kiss her hand twice, and with a look of sensibility mixed with a concern she got out of the chaise—and bid adieu.

IN THE STREET.
CALAIS.

I NEVER finished a twelve-guinea bargain so expeditiously in my life: my time seemed heavy upon the loss of the lady, and knowing every moment of it would be as two, till I put myself into motion—I ordered post horses directly, and walked towards the hotel.

Lord! said I, hearing the town clock strike four, and recollecting that I had been little more than a single hour in Calais—

—What a large volume of adventures may be grasped within this little span of life by him who interests his heart in every thing, and who, having eyes to see, what time and chance are perpetually holding out to him as he journeyeth on his way, misses nothing he can *fairly* lay his hands on.—[48]

—If this won't turn out something—another will—no matter—'tis an assay upon human nature—I get my labour for my pains—'tis enough—the pleasure of the experiment has kept my senses, and the best part of my blood awake, and laid the gross to sleep.

I pity the man who can travel from *Dan* to *Beersheba*,[49] and cry, 'Tis all barren—and so it is; and so is all the world to him who will not cultivate the fruits it offers. I declare, said I, clapping my hands chearily together, that was I in a desart, I would find out wherewith in it to call forth my affections—If I could not do better, I would fasten them upon some sweet myrtle, or seek some melancholy cypress to connect myself to— I would court their shade, and greet them kindly for their protection— I would cut my name upon them, and swear they were the loveliest trees throughout the desart: if their leaves wither'd, I would teach myself to mourn, and when they rejoiced, I would rejoice along with them.

The learned SMELFUNGUS[50] travelled from Boulogne to Paris— from Paris to Rome—and so on—but he set out with the spleen and jaundice, and every object he pass'd by was discoloured or distorted— He wrote an account of them, but 'twas nothing but the account of his miserable feelings.

I met Smelfungus in the grand portico of the Pantheon—he was just coming out of it—*'Tis nothing but a huge cock-pit**, said he—I wish you had said nothing worse of the Venus of Medicis, replied I—for in passing through Florence, I had heard he had fallen foul upon the goddess, and used her worse than a common strumpet, without the least provocation in nature.[51]

I popp'd upon Smelfungus again at Turin, in his return home; and a sad tale of sorrowful adventures had he to tell, "wherein he spoke of moving accidents by flood and field, and of the cannibals which each other eat: the Anthropophagi"[52]—he had been flea'd alive, and bedevil'd, and used worse than St. Bartholomew, at every stage he had come at—[53]

—I'll tell it, cried Smelfungus, to the world. You had better tell it, said I, to your physician.

Mundungus, with an immense fortune, made the whole tour; going on from Rome to Naples—from Naples to Venice—from Venice to Vienna—to Dresden, to Berlin, without one generous connection or pleasurable anecdote to tell of; but he had travell'd straight on looking neither to his right hand or his left, lest Love or Pity should seduce him out of his road.[54]

Peace be to them! if it is to be found; but heaven itself, was it possible to get there with such tempers, would want objects to give it—every gentle spirit would come flying upon the wings of Love to hail their arrival—Nothing would the souls of Smelfungus and Mundungus hear of, but fresh anthems of joy, fresh raptures of love, and fresh congratulations of their common felicity—I heartily pity them: they have brought up no faculties for this work; and was the happiest mansion in heaven to be allotted to Smelfungus and Mundungus, they would be so far from being happy, that the souls of Smelfungus and Mundungus would do penance there to all eternity.

* Vide S——'s Travels.

MONTRIUL.

I HAD once lost my portmanteau from behind my chaise, and twice got out in the rain, and one of the times up to the knees in dirt, to help the postilion to tie it on, without being able to find out what was wanting—Nor was it till I got to Montriul, upon the landlord's asking me if I wanted not a servant, that it occurred to me, that that was the very thing.

A servant! That I do most sadly, quoth I—Because, Monsieur, said the landlord, there is a clever young fellow, who would be very proud of the honour to serve an Englishman—But why an English one, more than any other?—They are so generous, said the landlord—I'll be shot if this is not a livre out of my pocket, quoth I to myself, this very night—But they have wherewithal to be so, Monsieur, added he—Set down one livre more for that, quoth I—It was but last night, said the landlord, *qu'un my Lord Anglois presentoit un ecu a la fille de chambre—Tant pis, pour Mad^{lle} Janatone,*[55] said I.

Now Janatone being the landlord's daughter, and the landlord supposing I was young in French, took the liberty to inform me, I should not have said *tant pis*—but, *tant mieux. Tant mieux, toujours, Monsieur*, said he, when there is any thing to be got—*tant pis*, when there is nothing. It comes to the same thing, said I. *Pardonnez moi*,[56] said the landlord.

I cannot take a fitter opportunity to observe once for all, that *tant pis* and *tant mieux* being two of the great hinges in French conversation, a stranger would do well to set himself right in the use of them, before he gets to Paris.

A prompt French Marquis at our ambassador's table demanded of Mr. H——, if he was H—— the poet? No, said H—— mildly—*Tant pis*, replied the Marquis.

It is H—— the historian, said another—*Tant mieux*, said the Marquis. And Mr. H——, who is a man of an excellent heart, return'd thanks for both.[57]

When the landlord had set me right in this matter, he called in

La Fleur, which was the name of the young man he had spoke of—saying only first, That as for his talents, he would presume to say nothing—Monsieur was the best judge what would suit him; but for the fidelity of La Fleur, he would stand responsible in all he was worth.

The landlord deliver'd this in a manner which instantly set my mind to the business I was upon—and La Fleur, who stood waiting without, in that breathless expectation which every son of nature of us have felt in our turns, came in.

MONTRIUL.

I AM apt to be taken with all kinds of people at first sight; but never more so, than when a poor devil comes to offer his service to so poor a devil as myself; and as I know this weakness, I always suffer my judgment to draw back something on that very account—and this more or less, according to the mood I am in, and the case—and I may add the gender too, of the person I am to govern.

When La Fleur enter'd the room, after every discount I could make for my soul, the genuine look and air of the fellow determined the matter at once in his favour; so I hired him first—and then began to inquire what he could do: But I shall find out his talents, quoth I, as I want them—besides, a Frenchman can do every thing.

Now poor La Fleur could do nothing in the world but beat a drum, and play a march or two upon the fife. I was determined to make his talents do; and can't say my weakness was ever so insulted by my wisdom, as in the attempt.

La Fleur had set out early in life, as gallantly as most Frenchmen do, with *serving* for a few years; at the end of which, having satisfied the sentiment, and found moreover, That the honour of beating a drum was likely to be its own reward, as it open'd no further track of glory to him—he retired *a ses terres*, and lived *comme il plaisoit a Dieu*[58]—that is to say, upon nothing.

—And so, quoth *Wisdome*, you have hired a drummer to attend you
in this tour of your's thro' France and Italy! Psha! said I, and do not
one half of our gentry go with a hum-drum *compagnon du voiage* the
same round, and have the piper and the devil and all to pay besides?
When man can extricate himself with an *equivoque* in such an unequal
match—he is not ill off—But you can do something else, La Fleur?
said I——*O qu'oui!*[59]—he could make spatterdashes,[60] and play a little
upon the fiddle—Bravo! said Wisdome—Why, I play a bass myself,
said I—we shall do very well.—You can shave, and dress a wig a little,
La Fleur?—He had all the dispositions in the world—It is enough for
heaven! said I, interrupting him—and ought to be enough for me—
So supper coming in, and having a frisky English spaniel on one side
of my chair, and a French valet, with as much hilarity in his countenance as ever nature painted in one, on the other—I was satisfied to my
heart's content with my empire; and if monarchs knew what they
would be at, they might be as satisfied as I was.

MONTRIUL.

AS La Fleur went the whole tour of France and Italy with me, and
will be often upon the stage, I must interest the reader a little
further in his behalf, by saying, that I had never less reason to repent
of the impulses which generally do determine me, than in regard to
this fellow—he was a faithful, affectionate, simple soul as ever trudged
after the heels of a philosopher; and notwithstanding his talents
of drum-beating and spatterdash-making, which, tho' very good in
themselves, happen'd to be of no great service to me, yet was I
hourly recompenced by the festivity of his temper—it supplied all
defects—I had a constant resource in his looks in all difficulties and
distresses of my own—I was going to have added, of his too; but La
Fleur was out of the reach of every thing; for whether 'twas hunger
or thirst, or cold or nakedness, or watchings, or whatever stripes of
ill luck La Fleur met with in our journeyings,[61] there was no index

in his physiognomy to point them out by—he was eternally the same; so that if I am a piece of a philosopher, which Satan now and then puts it into my head I am—it always mortifies the pride of the conceit, by reflecting how much I owe to the complexional philosophy of this poor fellow, for shaming me into one of a better kind. With all this, La Fleur had a small cast of the coxcomb—but he seemed at first sight to be more a coxcomb of nature than of art; and before I had been three days in Paris with him—he seemed to be no coxcomb at all.

MONTRIUL.

THE next morning La Fleur entering upon his employment, I delivered to him the key of my portmanteau with an inventory of my half a dozen shirts and silk pair of breeches; and bid him fasten all upon the chaise—get the horses put to—and desire the landlord to come in with his bill.

C'est un garçon de bonne fortune,[62] said the landlord, pointing through the window to half a dozen wenches who had got round about La Fleur, and were most kindly taking their leave of him, as the postilion was leading out the horses. La Fleur kissed all their hands round and round again, and thrice he wiped his eyes, and thrice he promised he would bring them all pardons from Rome.

The young fellow, said the landlord, is beloved by all the town, and there is scarce a corner in Montriul where the want of him will not be felt: he has but one misfortune in the world, continued he, "He is always in love."—I am heartily glad of it, said I,—'twill save me the trouble every night of putting my breeches under my head. In saying this, I was making not so much La Fleur's eloge,[63] as my own, having been in love with one princess or another almost all my life, and I hope I shall go on so, till I die, being firmly persuaded, that if ever I do a mean action, it must be in some interval betwixt one passion and another: whilst this interregnum lasts, I always perceive my heart locked up—I can scarce find in it, to give Misery a sixpence; and therefore I always get out of it as fast as I can, and the moment I am rekindled, I am all generosity and good will again; and would do any thing in the world either for, or with any one, if they will but satisfy me there is no sin in it.

—But in saying this—surely I am commending the passion—not myself.

A FRAGMENT.

——— THE town of Abdera, notwithstanding Democritus lived there trying all the powers of irony and laughter to reclaim it,[64] was the vilest and most profligate town in all Thrace. What for poisons, conspiracies and assassinations—libels, pasquinades[65] and tumults, there was no going there by day—'twas worse by night.

Now, when things were at the worst, it came to pass, that the Andromeda of Euripides[66] being represented at Abdera, the whole orchestra[67] was delighted with it: but of all the passages which delighted them, nothing operated more upon their imaginations, than the tender strokes of nature which the poet had wrought up in that pathetic speech of Perseus,

O Cupid, prince of God and men, &c.

Every man almost spoke pure iambics the next day, and talk'd of nothing but Perseus his pathetic address—"O Cupid! prince of God and men"—in every street of Abdera, in every house—"O Cupid! Cupid!"—in every mouth, like the natural notes of some sweet melody which drops from it whether it will or no—nothing but "Cupid! Cupid! prince of God and men"—The fire caught—and the whole city, like the heart of one man, open'd itself to Love.

No pharmacopolist could sell one grain of helebore[68]—not a single armourer had a heart to forge one instrument of death—Friendship and Virtue met together, and kiss'd each other in the street—the golden age return'd, and hung o'er the town of Abdera—every Abderite took his oaten pipe, and every Abderitish woman left her purple web, and chastly sat her down and listen'd to the song—

'Twas only in the power, says the Fragment, of the God whose empire extendeth from heaven to earth, and even to the depths of the sea, to have done this.

MONTRIUL.

WHEN all is ready, and every article is disputed and paid for in the inn, unless you are a little sour'd by the adventure, there is always a matter to compound at the door, before you can get into your chaise; and that is with the sons and daughters of poverty, who surround you. Let no man say, "let them go to the devil"—'tis a cruel journey to send a few miserables, and they have had sufferings enow without it: I always think it better to take a few sous out in my hand; and I would counsel every gentle traveller to do so likewise: he need not be so exact in setting down his motives for giving them—they will be register'd elsewhere.

For my own part, there is no man gives so little as I do; for few that I know have so little to give: but as this was the first publick act of my charity in France, I took the more notice of it.

A well-a-way! said I. I have but eight sous in the world, shewing them in my hand, and there are eight poor men and eight poor women for 'em.

A poor tatter'd soul without a shirt on instantly withdrew his claim, by retiring two steps out of the circle, and making a disqualifying bow on his part. Had the whole parterre cried out, *Place aux dames*,[69] with one voice, it would not have conveyed the sentiment of a deference for the sex with half the effect.

Just heaven! for what wise reasons hast thou order'd it, that beggary and urbanity, which are at such variance in other countries, should find a way to be at unity in this?

—I insisted upon presenting him with a single sous, merely for his *politesse*.

A poor little dwarfish brisk fellow, who stood over-against me in the circle, putting something first under his arm, which had once been a hat, took his snuff-box out of his pocket, and generously offer'd a pinch on both sides of him: it was a gift of consequence, and modestly declined—The poor little fellow press'd it upon them with a nod of welcomeness—*Prenez en—prenez*,[70] said he, looking another way; so they each took a pinch—Pity thy box should ever want one! said I to myself; so I put a couple of sous into it—taking a small pinch out of his box, to enhance their value, as I did it—He felt the weight of the second obligation more than that of the first—'twas doing him an honour—the other was only doing him a charity—and he made me a bow down to the ground for it.

—Here! said I to an old soldier with one hand, who had been campaign'd and worn out to death in the service—here's a couple of sous for thee—*Vive le Roi!* said the old soldier.

I had then but three sous left: so I gave one, simply *pour l'amour de Dieu*, which was the footing on which it was begg'd—The poor woman had a dislocated hip; so it could not be well, upon any other motive.

Mon cher et tres charitable Monsieur—There's no opposing this, said I.

My Lord Anglois—the very sound was worth the money—so I gave *my last sous for it.* But in the eagerness of giving, I had overlook'd a *pauvre honteux*,[71] who had no one to ask a sous for him, and who, I believed, would have perish'd, ere he could have ask'd one for himself: he stood by the chaise a little without the circle, and wiped a tear from a face which I thought had seen better days—Good God! said I—and I have not one single sous left to give him—But you have a thousand! cried all the powers of nature, stirring within me—so I gave him—no matter what—I am ashamed to say *how much*, now—and was ashamed to think, how little, then: so if the reader can form any conjecture of my disposition, as these two fixed points are given him, he may judge within a livre or two what was the precise sum.

I could afford nothing for the rest, but, *Dieu vous benisse—Et le bon Dieu vous benisse encore*[72]—said the old soldier, the dwarf, &c. The *pauvre honteux* could say nothing—he pull'd out a little handkerchief, and wiped his face as he turned away—and I thought he thank'd me more than them all.

THE BIDET.

HAVING settled all these little matters, I got into my post-chaise with more ease than ever I got into a post-chaise in my life; and La Fleur having got one large jack-boot on the far side of a little *bidet**, and another on this (for I count nothing of his legs)—he canter'd away before me as happy and as perpendicular as a prince.—

—But what is happiness! what is grandeur in this painted scene of life! A dead ass, before we had got a league, put a sudden stop to La Fleur's career—his bidet would not pass by it—a contention arose betwixt them, and the poor fellow was kick'd out of his jack-boots the very first kick.

La Fleur bore his fall like a French christian, saying neither more or less upon it, than, Diable! so presently got up and came to the charge again astride his bidet, beating him up to it as he would have beat his drum.

The bidet flew from one side of the road to the other, then back again—then this way—then that way, and in short every way but by the dead ass.—La Fleur insisted upon the thing—and the bidet threw him.

What's the matter, La Fleur, said I, with this bidet of thine?— *Monsieur*, said he, *c'est un cheval le plus opiniâtré du monde*—Nay, if he is a conceited beast, he must go his own way, replied I—so La Fleur got off him, and giving him a good sound lash, the bidet took me at my word, and away he scamper'd back to Montriul.—*Peste!* said La Fleur.

It is not *mal a propos*[73] to take notice here, that tho' La Fleur availed himself but of two different terms of exclamation in this encounter— namely, *Diable!* and *Peste!* that there are nevertheless three, in the

---

* Post horse.

French language; like the positive, comparative, and superlative, one or the other of which serve for every unexpected throw of the dice in life.

Le Diable! which is the first, and positive degree, is generally used upon ordinary emotions of the mind, where small things only fall out contrary to your expectations—such as—the throwing once doublets[74]—La Fleur's being kick'd off his horse, and so forth—cuckoldom, for the same reason, is always—*Le Diable!*

But in cases where the cast[75] has something provoking in it, as in that of the bidet's running away after, and leaving La Fleur aground in jack-boots—'tis the second degree.

'Tis then *Peste!*

And for the third—[76]

—But here my heart is wrung with pity and fellow-feeling, when I reflect what miseries must have been their lot, and how bitterly so refined a people must have smarted, to have forced them upon the use of it.—

Grant me, O ye powers which touch the tongue with eloquence in distress!—whatever is my *cast*, Grant me but decent words to exclaim in, and I will give my nature way.

—But as these were not to be had in France, I resolved to take every evil just as it befell me without any exclamation at all.

La Fleur, who had made no such covenant with himself, followed the bidet with his eyes till it was got out of sight—and then, you may imagine, if you please, with what word he closed the whole affair.

As there was no hunting down a frighten'd horse in jack-boots, there remained no alternative but taking La Fleur either behind the chaise, or into it.—

I preferred the latter, and in half an hour we got to the post-house at Nampont.

Starts.

↑ In the midde of things

NAMPONT.
THE DEAD ASS.

—AND this, said he, putting the remains of a crust into his wallet— and this, should have been thy portion, said he, hadst thou been alive to have shared it with me. I thought by the accent, it had been an apostrophe to his child; but 'twas to his ass, and to the very ass we had seen dead in the road, which had occasioned La Fleur's misadventure. The man seemed to lament it much; and it instantly brought into my mind Sancho's lamentation for his;[77] but he did it with more true touches of nature.

The mourner was sitting upon a stone bench at the door, with the ass's pannel[78] and its bridle on one side, which he took up from time to time—then laid them down—look'd at them and shook his head. He then took his crust of bread out of his wallet again, as if to eat it; held it some time in his hand—then laid it upon the bit of his ass's bridle—looked wistfully at the little arrangement he had made—and then gave a sigh.

The simplicity of his grief drew numbers about him, and La Fleur amongst the rest, whilst the horses were getting ready; as I continued sitting in the post-chaise, I could see and hear over their heads.

—He said he had come last from Spain, where he had been from the furthest borders of Franconia; and had got so far on his return home, when his ass died. Every one seem'd desirous to know what business could have taken so old and poor a man so far a journey from his own home.

It had pleased heaven, he said, to bless him with three sons, the finest lads in all Germany; but having in one week lost two of the eldest of them by the small-pox, and the youngest falling ill of the same distemper, he was afraid of being bereft of them all; and made a vow, if Heaven would not take him from him also, he would go in gratitude to St. Iago in Spain.[79]

When the mourner got thus far on his story, he stopp'd to pay nature her tribute—and wept bitterly.

He said, Heaven had accepted the conditions; and that he had set out from his cottage with this poor creature, who had been a patient partner of his journey—that it had eat the same bread with him all the way, and was unto him as a friend.[80]

Every body who stood about, heard the poor fellow with concern—
—La Fleur offered him money.—The mourner said, he did not want it—it was not the value of the ass—but the loss of him.—The ass, he said, he was assured loved him—and upon this told them a long story of a mischance upon their passage over the Pyrenean mountains which had separated them from each other three days; during which time the ass had sought him as much as he had sought the ass, and that they had neither scarce eat or drank till they met.

Thou hast one comfort, friend, said I, at least in the loss of thy poor beast; I'm sure thou hast been a merciful master to him.—Alas! said the mourner, I thought so, when he was alive—but now that he is dead I think otherwise.—I fear the weight of myself and my afflictions together have been too much for him—they have shortened the poor creature's days, and I fear I have them to answer for.—Shame on the world! said I to myself—Did we love each other, as this poor soul but loved his ass—'twould be something.—

NAMPONT.
THE POSTILLION.

THE concern which the poor fellow's story threw me into, required some attention: the postillion paid not the least to it, but set off upon the *pavè*[81] in a full gallop.

The thirstiest soul in the most sandy desert of Arabia could not have wished more for a cup of cold water,[82] than mine did for grave and quiet movements; and I should have had an high opinion of the postillion had he but stolen off with me in something like a pensive pace.—On the contrary, as the mourner finished his lamentation, the fellow gave an unfeeling lash to each of his beasts, and set off clattering like a thousand devils.

I called to him as loud as I could, for heaven's sake to go slower—and the louder I called the more unmercifully he galloped.—The deuce take him and his galloping too—said I—he'll go on tearing my nerves to pieces till he has worked me into a foolish passion, and then he'll go slow, that I may enjoy the sweets of it.

The postillion managed the point to a miracle: by the time he had got to the foot of a steep hill about half a league from Nampont,—he had put me out of temper with him—and then with myself, for being so.

My case then required a different treatment; and a good rattling gallop would have been of real service to me.—

—Then, prithee get on—get on, my good lad, said I.

The postillion pointed to the hill—I then tried to return back to the story of the poor German and his ass—but I had broke the clue[83]—and could no more get into it again, than the postillion could into a trot.—

—The deuce go, said I, with it all! Here am I sitting as candidly disposed to make the best of the worst, as ever wight was, and all runs counter.

There is one sweet lenitive at least for evils, which nature holds out to us; so I took it kindly at her hands, and fell asleep; and the first word which roused me was *Amiens*.

—Bless me! said I, rubbing my eyes—this is the very town where my poor lady is to come.

AMIENS.

THE words were scarce out of my mouth, when the Count de L***'s post-chaise, with his sister in it, drove hastily by: she had just time to make me a bow of recognition—and of that particular kind of it, which told me she had not yet done with me. She was as good as her look; for, before I had quite finished my supper, her brother's servant came into the room with a billet, in which she said, she had taken the liberty to charge me with a letter, which I was to present myself to Madame R*** the first morning I had nothing to do at Paris. There was only added, she was sorry, but from what *penchant* she had not considered, that she had been prevented telling me her story— that she still owed it me; and if my rout should ever lay through Brussels, and I had not by then forgot the name of Madame de L***— that Madame de L*** would be glad to discharge her obligation.

Then I will meet thee, said I, fair spirit! at Brussels—'tis only returning from Italy through Germany to Holland, by the rout of Flanders, home—'twill scarce be ten posts out of my way; but were it ten thousand! with what a moral delight will it crown my journey, in sharing in the sickening incidents of a tale of misery told to me by such a sufferer? to see her weep! and though I cannot dry up the fountain of her tears, what an exquisite sensation is there still left, in wiping them away from off the cheeks of the first and fairest of women,[84] as I'm sitting with my handkerchief in my hand in silence the whole night besides her.

There was nothing wrong in the sentiment; and yet I instantly reproached my heart with it in the bitterest and most reprobate of expressions.

It had ever, as I told the reader, been one of the singular blessings of my life, to be almost every hour of it miserably in love with some one; and my last flame happening to be blown out by a whiff of jealousy on the sudden turn of a corner, I had lighted it up afresh at the pure taper of Eliza but about three months before—swearing as I did it, that it should last me through the whole journey—Why should I dissemble the matter? I had sworn to her eternal fidelity—she had a right to my whole heart—to divide my affections was to lessen them— to expose them, was to risk them: where there is risk, there may be loss—and what wilt thou have, Yorick! to answer to a heart so full of trust and confidence—so good, so gentle and unreproaching?

—I will not go to Brussels, replied I, interrupting myself—but my imagination went on—I recall'd her looks at that crisis of our separation when neither of us had power to say Adieu! I look'd at the picture she had tied in a black ribband about my neck—and blush'd as I look'd at it—I would have given the world to have kiss'd it,—but was ashamed—And shall this tender flower, said I, pressing it between my hands—shall it be smitten to its very root—and smitten, Yorick! by thee, who hast promised to shelter it in thy breast?

Eternal fountain of happiness! said I, kneeling down upon the ground—be thou my witness—and every pure spirit which tastes it, be my witness also, That I would not travel to Brussels, unless Eliza went along with me, did the road lead me towards heaven.

In transports of this kind, the heart, in spite of the understanding, will always say too much.

THE LETTER.
AMIENS.

FORTUNE had not smiled upon La Fleur; for he had been unsuccessful in his feats of chivalry—and not one thing had offer'd to signalize his zeal for my service from the time he had enter'd into it, which was almost four and twenty hours. The poor soul burn'd with impatience; and the Count de L***'s servant's coming with the letter, being the first practicable occasion which offered, La Fleur had laid hold of it; and in order to do honour to his master, had taken him into a back parlour in the Auberge, and treated him with a cup or two of the best wine in Picardy; and the Count de L***'s servant in return, and not to be behind hand in politeness with La Fleur, had taken him back with him to the Count's hôtel.[85] La Fleur's *prevenancy*[86] (for there was a passport in his very looks) soon set every servant in the kitchen at ease with him; and as a Frenchman, whatever be his talents, has no sort of prudery in shewing them, La Fleur, in less than five minutes, had pull'd out his fife, and leading off the dance himself with the first note, set the *fille de chambre*, the *maitre d'hotel*,[87] the cook, the scullion, and all the houshold, dogs and cats, besides an old monkey, a-dancing: I suppose there never was a merrier kitchen since the flood.

Madame de L***, in passing from her brother's apartments to her own, hearing so much jollity below stairs, rung up her *fille de chambre* to ask about it; and hearing it was the English gentleman's servant who had set the whole house merry with his pipe, she order'd him up.

As the poor fellow could not present himself empty, he had loaden'd himself in going up stairs with a thousand compliments to Madame de L***, on the part of his master—added a long apocrypha of inquiries after Madame de L***'s health—told her, that Monsieur his master was *au desespoire*[88] for her re-establishment from the fatigues of her journey—and, to close all, that Monsieur had received the letter which Madame had done him the honour——And he had done me the honour, said Madame de L***, interrupting La Fleur, to send a billet in return.

Madame de L*** had said this with such a tone of reliance upon the fact, that La Fleur had not power to disappoint her expectations— he trembled for my honour—and possibly might not altogether be unconcerned for his own, as a man capable of being attach'd to a master who could be a wanting *en egards vis a vis d'une femme*;[89] so that when Madame de L*** asked La Fleur if he had brought a letter—*O qu'oui*, said La Fleur: so laying down his hat upon the ground, and taking hold of the flap of his right side pocket with his left hand, he began to search for the letter with his right—then contrary-wise—*Diable!*—then sought every pocket—pocket by pocket, round, not forgetting his fob—*Peste!*—then La Fleur emptied them upon the floor—pulled out a dirty cravat—a handkerchief—a comb—a whip lash—a night-cap— then gave a peep into his hat—*Quelle etourderie!*[90] He had left the letter upon the table in the Auberge—he would run for it, and be back with it in three minutes.

I had just finished my supper when La Fleur came in to give me an account of his adventure: he told the whole story simply as it was; and only added, that if Monsieur had forgot (*par hazard*) to answer Madame's letter, the arrangement gave him an opportunity to recover the *faux pas*[91]—and if not, that things were only as they were.

Now I was not altogether sure of my *etiquette*, whether I ought to have wrote or no; but if I had—a devil himself could not have been angry: 'twas but the officious zeal of a well-meaning creature for my honour; and however he might have mistook the road—or embarrassed me in so doing—his heart was in no fault—I was under no necessity to write—and what weighed more than all—he did not look as if he had done amiss.

—'Tis all very well, La Fleur, said I.—'Twas sufficient. La Fleur flew out of the room like lightening, and return'd with pen, ink, and paper, in his hand; and coming up to the table, laid them close before me, with such a delight in his countenance, that I could not help taking up the pen.

I begun and begun again; and though I had nothing to say, and that nothing might have been express'd in half a dozen lines, I made half a dozen different beginnings, and could no way please myself.

In short, I was in no mood to write.

La Fleur stepp'd out and brought a little water in a glass to dilute my ink—then fetch'd sand and seal-wax—It was all one: I wrote, and blotted, and tore off, and burnt, and wrote again—*Le Diable l'emporte!*[92] said I half to myself—I cannot write this self-same letter; throwing the pen down despairingly as I said it.

As soon as I had cast down the pen, La Fleur advanced with the most respectful carriage up to the table, and making a thousand apologies for the liberty he was going to take, told me he had a letter in his pocket wrote by a drummer in his regiment to a corporal's wife, which, he durst say, would suit the occasion.

I had a mind to let the poor fellow have his humour—Then prithee, said I, let me see it.

La Fleur instantly pull'd out a little dirty pocket-book cramm'd full of small letters and billet-doux in a sad condition, and laying it upon the table, and then untying the string which held them all together, run them over one by one, till he came to the letter in question—*La voila!*[93] said he, clapping his hands: so unfolding it first, he laid it before me, and retired three steps from the table whilst I read it.

THE LETTER.

MADAME,

JE suis penetré de la douleur la plus vive, et reduit en même temps au desespoir par ce retour imprevû du Corporal qui rend notre entrevue de ce soir la chose du monde la plus impossible.

Mais vive la joie! et toute la mienne sera de penser a vous.

L'amour n'est *rien* sans sentiment.

Et le sentiment est encore *moins* sans amour.

On dit qu'on ne doit jamais se desesperer.

On dit aussi que Monsieur le Corporal monte la garde Mecredi: alors ce sera mon tour.

Chacun a son tour.

En attendant—Vive l'amour! et vive la bagatelle!

Je suis, MADAME,

Avec toutes les sentiments les plus respecteux et les plus tendres tout a vous,[94]

JAQUES ROQUE.

It was but changing the Corporal into the Count—and saying nothing about mounting guard on Wednesday—and the letter was neither right or wrong—so to gratify the poor fellow, who stood trembling for my honour, his own, and the honour of his letter,—I took the cream gently off it, and whipping it up in my own way—I seal'd it up and sent him with it to Madame de L***—and the next morning we pursued our journey to Paris.

This is its own section

PARIS.

W HEN a man can contest the point by dint of equipage, and carry all on floundering before him with half a dozen lackies and a couple of cooks—'tis very well in such a place as Paris—he may drive in at which end of a street he will.

A poor prince who is weak in cavalry, and whose whole infantry does not exceed a single man, had best quit the field; and signalize himself in the cabinet,[95] if he can get up into it—I say *up into it*—for there is no descending perpendicular amongst 'em with a "*Me voici! mes enfans*"[96]—here I am—whatever many may think.

I own my first sensations, as soon as I was left solitary and alone in my own chamber in the hotel, were far from being so flattering as I had prefigured them. I walked up gravely to the window in my dusty black coat, and looking through the glass saw all the world in yellow, blue, and green, running at the ring of pleasure.—The old with broken lances, and in helmets which had lost their vizards—the young in armour bright which shone like gold, beplumed with each gay feather of the east—all—all tilting at it like fascinated knights in tournaments of yore for fame and love.—[97]

Alas, poor Yorick![98] cried I, what art thou doing here? On the very first onset of all this glittering clatter, thou art reduced to an atom—seek—seek some winding alley, with a tourniquet at the end of it, where chariot never rolled or flambeau[99] shot its rays—there thou mayest solace thy soul in converse sweet with some kind *grisset*[100] of a barber's wife, and get into such coteries!—

—May I perish! if I do, said I, pulling out the letter which I had to present to Madame de R***.—I'll wait upon this lady, the very first thing I do. So I called La Fleur to go seek me a barber directly—and come back and brush my coat.

THE WIG.
PARIS.

WHEN the barber came, he absolutely refused to have any thing to do with my wig: 'twas either above or below his art: I had nothing to do, but to take one ready made of his own recommendation.

—But I fear, friend! said I, this buckle[101] won't stand.—You may immerge it, replied he, into the ocean, and it will stand—

What a great scale is every thing upon in this city! thought I—The utmost stretch of an English periwig-maker's ideas could have gone no further than to have "dipped it into a pail of water"—What difference! 'tis like time to eternity.

I confess I do hate all cold conceptions, as I do the puny ideas which engender them; and am generally so struck with the great works of nature, that for my own part, if I could help it, I never would make a comparison less than a mountain at least. All that can be said against the French sublime in this instance of it, is this—that the grandeur is *more* in the *word*; and *less* in the *thing*. No doubt the ocean fills the mind with vast ideas; but Paris being so far inland, it was not likely I should run post a hundred miles out of it, to try the experiment—the Parisian barber meant nothing.—

The pail of water standing besides the great deep, makes certainly but a sorry figure in speech—but 'twill be said—it has one advantage—'tis in the next room, and the truth of the buckle may be tried in it without more ado, in a single moment.

In honest truth, and upon a more candid revision of the matter, *The French expression professes more than it performs.*

I think I can see the precise and distinguishing marks of national characters more in these nonsensical *minutiæ*, than in the most important matters of state; where great men of all nations talk and stalk so much alike, that I would not give nine-pence to chuse amongst them.

I was so long in getting from under my barber's hands, that it was too late to think of going with my letter to Madame R*** that night:

but when a man is once dressed at all points for going out, his reflections turn to little account, so taking down the name of the Hotel de Modene where I lodged, I walked forth without any determination where to go—I shall consider of that, said I, as I walk along.

THE PULSE.
PARIS.

HAIL ye small sweet courtesies of life, for smooth do ye make the road of it! like grace and beauty which beget inclinations to love at first sight; 'tis ye who open this door and let the stranger in.

—Pray, Madame, said I, have the goodness to tell me which way I must turn to go to the Opera comique:—Most willingly, Monsieur, said she, laying aside her work—

I had given a cast with my eye into half a dozen shops as I came along in search of a face not likely to be disordered by such an interruption; till at last, this hitting my fancy, I had walked in.

She was working a pair of ruffles as she sat in a low chair on the far side of the shop facing the door—

—*Tres volentieres*; most willingly, said she, laying her work down upon a chair next her, and rising up from the low chair she was sitting in, with so chearful a movement and so chearful a look, that had I been laying out fifty louis d'ors with her, I should have said—"This woman is grateful."

You must turn, Monsieur, said she, going with me to the door of the shop, and pointing the way down the street I was to take—you must turn first to your left hand—*mais prenez guarde*[102]—there are two turns; and be so good as to take the second—then go down a little way and you'll see a church, and when you are past it, give yourself the trouble to turn directly to the right, and that will lead you to the foot of the *pont neuf*, which you must cross—and there, any one will do himself the pleasure to shew you—

She repeated her instructions three times over to me with the same good natur'd patience the third time as the first;—and if *tones and manners* have a meaning, which certainly they have, unless to hearts which shut them out[103]—she seem'd really interested, that I should not lose myself.

I will not suppose it was the woman's beauty, notwithstanding she was the handsomest grisset, I think, I ever saw, which had much to do with the sense I had of her courtesy; only I remember, when I told her how much I was obliged to her, that I looked very full in her eyes,— and that I repeated my thanks as often as she had done her instructions.

I had not got ten paces from the door, before I found I had forgot every tittle of what she had said—so looking back, and seeing her still standing in the door of the shop as if to look whether I went right or not—I returned back, to ask her whether the first turn was to my right or left—for that I had absolutely forgot.—Is it possible! said she, half laughing.—'Tis very possible, replied I, when a man is thinking more of a woman, than of her good advice.

As this was the real truth—she took it, as every woman takes a matter of right, with a slight courtesy.

—*Attendez!*[104] said she, laying her hand upon my arm to detain me, whilst she called a lad out of the back-shop to get ready a parcel of gloves. I am just going to send him, said she, with a packet into that quarter, and if you will have the complaisance to step in, it will be ready in a moment, and he shall attend you to the place.—So I walk'd in with her to the far side of the shop, and taking up the ruffle in my hand which she laid upon the chair, as if I had a mind to sit, she sat down herself in her low chair, and I instantly sat myself down besides her.

—He will be ready, Monsieur, said she, in a moment—And in that moment, replied I, most willingly would I say something very civil to you for all these courtesies. Any one may do a casual act of good nature, but a continuation of them shews it is a part of the temperature; and certainly, added I, if it is the same blood which comes from the heart, which descends to the extremes (touching her wrist) I am sure you must have one of the best pulses of any woman in the world— Feel it, said she, holding out her arm. So laying down my hat, I took hold of her fingers in one hand, and applied the two fore-fingers of my other to the artery—

—Would to heaven! my dear Eugenius,[105] thou hadst passed by, and beheld me sitting in my black coat, and in my lack-a-day-sical manner, counting the throbs of it, one by one, with as much true devotion as if I had been watching the critical ebb or flow of her fever—How wouldst thou have laugh'd and moralized upon my new profession?—and thou shouldst have laugh'd and moralized on— Trust me, my dear Eugenius, I should have said, "there are worse occupations in this world *than feeling a woman's pulse.*"—But a Grisset's! thou wouldst have said—and in an open shop! Yorick—

—So much the better: for when my views are direct, Eugenius, I care not if all the world saw me feel it.

THE HUSBAND.
PARIS.

I HAD counted twenty pulsations, and was going on fast towards the fortieth, when her husband coming unexpected from a back parlour into the shop, put me a little out in my reckoning—'Twas no body but her husband, she said—so I began a fresh score—Monsieur is so good, quoth she, as he pass'd by us, as to give himself the trouble of feeling my pulse—The husband took off his hat, and making me a bow, said, I did him too much honour—and having said that, he put on his hat and walk'd out.

Good God! said I to myself, as he went out—and can this man be the husband of this woman?

Let it not torment the few who know what must have been the grounds of this exclamation, if I explain it to those who do not.

In London a shopkeeper and a shopkeeper's wife seem to be one bone and one flesh: in the several endowments of mind and body, sometimes the one, sometimes the other has it, so as in general to be

51

upon a par, and to tally with each other as nearly as man and wife need to do.

In Paris, there are scarce two orders of beings more different: for the legislative and executive powers of the shop not resting in the husband, he seldom comes there—in some dark and dismal room behind, he sits commerceless in his thrum night-cap,[106] the same rough son of Nature that Nature left him.

The genius of a people where nothing but the monarchy is *salique*,[107] having ceded this department, with sundry others, totally to the women—by a continual higgling with customers of all ranks and sizes from morning to night, like so many rough pebbles shook long together in a bag, by amicable collisions, they have worn down their asperities and sharp angles, and not only become round and smooth, but will receive, some of them, a polish like a brilliant—Monsieur *le Mari* is little better than the stone under your foot—

—Surely—surely man! it is not good for thee to sit alone[108]—thou wast made for social intercourse and gentle greetings, and this improvement of our natures from it, I appeal to, as my evidence.

—And how does it beat, Monsieur? said she.—With all the benignity, said I, looking quietly in her eyes, that I expected—She was going to say something civil in return—but the lad came into the shop with the gloves—*A propos*, said I; I want a couple of pair myself.

THE GLOVES.
PARIS.

THE beautiful Grisset rose up when I said this, and going behind the counter, reach'd down a parcel and untied it: I advanced to the side over-against her: they were all too large. The beautiful Grisset measured them one by one across my hand—It would not alter the dimensions—She begg'd I would try a single pair, which seemed to be the least—She held it open—my hand slipp'd into it at once—It will not do, said I, shaking my head a little—No, said she, doing the same thing.

There are certain combined looks of simple subtlety—where whim, and sense, and seriousness, and nonsense, are so blended, that all the languages of Babel set loose together could not express them—they are communicated and caught so instantaneously, that you can scarce say which party is the infecter. I leave it to your men of words to swell pages about it—it is enough in the present to say again, the gloves would not do; so folding our hands within our arms, we both loll'd upon the counter—it was narrow, and there was just room for the parcel to lay between us.

The beautiful Grisset look'd sometimes at the gloves, then side-ways to the window, then at the gloves—and then at me. I was not disposed to break silence—I follow'd her example: so I look'd at the gloves, then to the window, then at the gloves, and then at her—and so on alternately.

I found I lost considerably in every attack—she had a quick black eye, and shot through two such long and silken eye-lashes with such penetration, that she look'd into my very heart and reins[109]—It may seem strange, but I could actually feel she did—

—It is no matter, said I, taking up a couple of the pairs next me, and putting them into my pocket.

I was sensible the beautiful Grisset had not ask'd above a single livre above the price—I wish'd she had ask'd a livre more, and was puzzling my brains how to bring the matter about—Do you think, my dear Sir, said she, mistaking my embarrassment, that I could ask a *sous* too much of a stranger—and of a stranger whose politeness, more than his want of gloves, has done me the honour to lay himself at my mercy?— *M'en croyez capable?*[110]—Faith! not I, said I; and if you were, you are welcome—So counting the money into her hand, and with a lower bow than one generally makes to a shopkeeper's wife, I went out, and her lad with his parcel followed me.

THE TRANSLATION.
PARIS.

THERE was no body in the box I was let into but a kindly old French officer. I love the character, not only because I honour the man whose manners are softened by a profession which makes bad men worse; but that I once knew one—for he is no more—and why should I not rescue one page from violation by writing his name in it, and telling the world it was Captain Tobias Shandy,[111] the dearest of my flock and friends, whose philanthropy I never think of at this long distance from his death—but my eyes gush out with tears. For his sake, I have a predilection for the whole corps of veterans; and so I strode over the two back rows of benches, and placed myself beside him.

The old officer was reading attentively a small pamphlet, it might be the book of the opera, with a large pair of spectacles. As soon as I sat down, he took his spectacles off, and putting them into a shagreen[112] case, return'd them and the book into his pocket together. I half rose up, and made him a bow.

Translate this into any civilized language in the world—the sense is this:

"Here's a poor stranger come in to the box—he seems as if he knew no body; and is never likely, was he to be seven years in Paris, if every man he comes near keeps his spectacles upon his nose—'tis shutting the door of conversation absolutely in his face—and using him worse than a German."

The French officer might as well have said it all aloud; and if he had, I should in course have put the bow I made him into French too, and told him, "I was sensible of his attention, and return'd him a thousand thanks for it."

There is not a secret so aiding to the progress of sociality, as to get master of this *short hand*, and be quick in rendering the several turns of looks and limbs, with all their inflections and delineations, into plain words. For my own part, by long habitude, I do it so mechanically, that when I walk the streets of London, I go translating all the way; and have more than once stood behind in the circle, where not three words have been said, and have brought off twenty different dialogues with me, which I could have fairly wrote down and sworn to.

I was going one evening to Martini's concert at Milan,[113] and was just entering the door of the hall, when the Marquesina di F*** was coming out in a sort of a hurry—she was almost upon me before I saw her; so I gave a spring to one side to let her pass—She had done the same, and on the same side too; so we ran our heads together: she instantly got to the other side to get out: I was just as unfortunate as she had been; for I had sprung to that side, and opposed her passage again—We both flew together to the other side, and then back—and so on—it was ridiculous; we both blush'd intolerably; so I did at last the thing I should have done at first—I stood stock still, and the Marquesina had no more difficulty. I had no power to go into the room, till I had made her so much reparation as to wait and follow her with my eye to the end of the passage—She look'd back twice, and walk'd along it rather side-ways, as if she would make room for any one coming up stairs to pass her—No, said I—that's a vile translation: the Marquesina has a right to the best apology I can make her; and that opening is left for me to do it in—so I ran and begg'd pardon for the embarrassment I had given her, saying it was my intention to have made her way. She answered, she was guided by the same intention towards me—so we reciprocally thank'd each other. She was at the top of the stairs; and seeing no *chichesbee*[114] near her, I begg'd to hand her to her coach—so we went down the stairs, stopping at every third step to talk of the concert and the adventure—Upon my word, Madame, said I when I had handed her in, I made six different efforts to let you go out—And I made six efforts, replied she, to let you enter—I wish to heaven you would make a seventh, said I—With all my heart, said she, making room—Life is too short to be long about the forms of it—so I instantly stepp'd in, and she carried me home with her—And what became of the concert, St. Cecilia,[115] who, I suppose, was at it, knows more than I.

I will only add, that the connection which arose out of that translation, gave me more pleasure than any one I had the honour to make in Italy.

THE DWARF.
PARIS.

I HAD never heard the remark made by any one in my life, except by one; and who that was,[116] will probably come out in this chapter; so that being pretty much unprepossessed, there must have been grounds for what struck me the moment I cast my eyes over the *parterre*—and that was, the unaccountable sport of nature in forming such numbers of dwarfs—No doubt, she sports at certain times in almost every corner of the world; but in Paris, there is no end to her amusements—The goddess seems almost as merry as she is wise.

As I carried my idea out of the *opera comique* with me, I measured every body I saw walking in the streets by it—Melancholy application! especially where the size was extremely little—the face extremely dark—the eyes quick—the nose long—the teeth white—the jaw prominent—to see so many miserables, by force of accidents driven out of their own proper class into the very verge of another, which it gives me pain to write down—every third man a pigmy!—some by ricketty heads and hump backs—others by bandy legs—a third set arrested by the hand of Nature in the sixth and seventh years of their growth—a fourth, in their perfect and natural state, like dwarf apple-trees; from the first rudiments and stamina of their existence, never meant to grow higher.

A medical traveller might say, 'tis owing to undue bandages—a splenetic one, to want of air—and an inquisitive traveller, to fortify the system, may measure the height of their houses—the narrowness of their streets, and in how few feet square in the sixth and seventh stories such numbers of the *Bourgoisie* eat and sleep together; but I remember, Mr. Shandy the elder,[117] who accounted for nothing like any body else, in speaking one evening of these matters, averred, that children, like other animals, might be increased almost to any size, provided they came right into the world; but the misery was, the citizens of Paris were so coop'd up, that they had not actually room enough to get them—I do not call it getting any thing, said he—'tis getting nothing—Nay, continued he, rising in his argument, 'tis getting worse than nothing, when all you have got, after twenty or five and twenty years of the tenderest care and most nutritious aliment bestowed upon it, shall not at last be as high as my leg. Now, Mr. Shandy being very short, there could be nothing more said upon it.

As this is not a work of reasoning, I leave the solution as I found it, and content myself with the truth only of the remark, which is verified in every lane and by-lane of Paris. I was walking down that which leads from the Carousal to the Palais Royal, and observing a little boy in some distress at the side of the gutter, which ran down the middle of it, I took hold of his hand, and help'd him over. Upon turning up his face to look at him after, I perceived he was about forty—Never mind, said I; some good body will do as much for me when I am ninety.

I feel some little principles within me, which incline me to be merciful towards this poor blighted part of my species, who have neither size or strength to get on in the world—I cannot bear to see one of them trod upon; and had scarce got seated beside my old French officer, ere the disgust was exercised, by seeing the very thing happen under the box we sat in.

At the end of the orchestra, and betwixt that and the first side-box, there is a small esplanade[118] left, where, when the house is full, numbers of all ranks take sanctuary. Though you stand, as in the parterre, you pay the same price as in the orchestra. A poor defenceless being of this order had got thrust some how or other into this luckless place—the night was hot, and he was surrounded by beings two feet and a half higher than himself. The dwarf suffered inexpressibly on all sides; but the thing which incommoded him most, was a tall corpulent German, near seven feet high, who stood directly betwixt him and all possibility of his seeing either the stage or the actors. The poor dwarf did all he could to get a peep at what was going forwards, by seeking for some little opening betwixt the German's arm and his body, trying first one side, then the other; but the German stood square in the most unaccommodating posture that can be imagined—the dwarf might as well have been placed at the bottom of the deepest draw-well in Paris; so he civilly reach'd up his hand to the German's sleeve, and told him his distress—The German turn'd his head back, look'd down upon him as Goliah did upon David—and unfeelingly resumed his posture.[119]

I was just then taking a pinch of snuff out of my monk's little horn box—And how would thy meek and courteous spirit, my dear monk! so temper'd to *bear and forbear!*—how sweetly would it have lent an ear to this poor soul's complaint!

The old French officer seeing me lift up my eyes with an emotion, as I made the apostrophe, took the liberty to ask me what was the matter—I told him the story in three words; and added, how inhuman it was.

By this time the dwarf was driven to extremes, and in his first transports, which are generally unreasonable, had told the German he would cut off his long queue[120] with his knife—The German look'd back coolly, and told him he was welcome if he could reach it.

An injury sharpened by an insult, be it to who it will, makes every man of sentiment a party: I could have leaped out of the box to have redressed it.—The old French officer did it with much less confusion; for leaning a little over, and nodding to a centinel,[121] and pointing at the same time with his finger to the distress—the centinel made his way up to it.—There was no occasion to tell the grievance—the thing told itself; so thrusting back the German instantly with his musket—he took the poor dwarf by the hand, and placed him before him.—This is noble! said I, clapping my hands together—And yet you would not permit this, said the old officer, in England.

—In England, dear Sir, said I, *we sit all at our ease.*

The old French officer would have set me at unity with myself, in case I had been at variance,—by saying it was a *bon mot*[122]—and as a *bon mot* is always worth something at Paris, he offered me a pinch of snuff.

THE ROSE.
PARIS.

IT was now my turn to ask the old French officer "What was the matter?" for a cry of "*Haussez les mains, Monsieur l'Abbe,*"[123] re-echoed from a dozen different parts of the parterre, was as unintelligible to me, as my apostrophe to the monk had been to him.

He told me, it was some poor Abbe in one of the upper loges, who he supposed had got planted perdu[124] behind a couple of grissets in order to see the opera, and that the parterre espying him, were insisting upon his holding up both his hands during the representation.—And can it be supposed, said I, that an ecclesiastick would pick the Grisset's pockets? The old French officer smiled, and whispering in my ear, open'd a door of knowledge which I had no idea of—

Good God! said I, turning pale with astonishment—is it possible, that a people so smit with sentiment should at the same time be so unclean, and so unlike themselves—*Quelle grossierte!*[125] added I.

The French officer told me, it was an illiberal sarcasm at the church, which had begun in the theatre about the time the Tartuffe was given in it, by Moliere—but, like other remains of Gothic manners, was declining—Every nation, continued he, have their refinements and *grossiertes*, in which they take the lead, and lose it of one another by turns—that he had been in most countries, but never in one where he found not some delicacies, which others seemed to want. *Le* POUR, *et le* CONTRE *se trouvent en chaque nation;*[126] there is a balance, said he, of good and bad every where; and nothing but the knowing it is so can emancipate one half of the world from the prepossessions which it holds against the other—that the advantage of travel, as it regarded the *sçavoir vivre,*[127] was by seeing a great deal both of men and manners; it taught us mutual toleration; and mutual toleration, concluded he, making me a bow, taught us mutual love.

The old French officer delivered this with an air of such candour and good sense, as coincided with my first favourable impressions of his character—I thought I loved the man; but I fear I mistook the object—'twas my own way of thinking—the difference was, I could not have expressed it half so well.

It is alike troublesome to both the rider and his beast—if the latter goes pricking up his ears, and starting all the way at every object which he never saw before—I have as little torment of this kind as any creature alive; and yet I honestly confess, that many a thing gave me pain, and that I blush'd at many a word the first month—which I found inconsequent and perfectly innocent the second.

Madame de Rambouliet,[128] after an acquaintance of about six weeks with her, had done me the honour to take me in her coach about two leagues out of town—Of all women, Madame de Rambouliet is the most correct; and I never wish to see one of more virtues and purity of heart—In our return back, Madame de Rambouliet desired me to pull the cord—I ask'd her if she wanted any thing—*Rien que pisser*,[129] said Madame de Rambouliet—

Grieve not, gentle traveller, to let Madame de Rambouliet p--ss on—And, ye fair mystic nymphs! go each one *pluck your rose*,[130] and scatter them in your path—for Madame de Rambouliet did no more— I handed Madame de Rambouliet out of the coach; and had I been the priest of the chaste Castalia,[131] I could not have served at her fountain with a more respectful decorum.

END OF VOL. I.

A

SENTIMENTAL JOURNEY

THROUGH

FRANCE AND ITALY.

BY

MR. YORICK.

VOL. II.

LONDON:

Printed for T. BECKET and P. A. DE HONDT,
in the Strand. MDCCLXVIII.

THE
FILLE DE CHAMBRE.
PARIS.

W HAT the old French officer had deliver'd upon travelling, bringing Polonius's advice to his son[1] upon the same subject into my head—and that bringing in Hamlet; and Hamlet, the rest of Shakespear's works, I stopp'd at the Quai de Conti in my return home, to purchase the whole set.

The bookseller said he had not a set in the world—*Comment!*[2] said I; taking one up out of a set which lay upon the counter betwixt us. —— He said, they were sent him only to be got bound, and were to be sent back to Versailles in the morning to the Count de B****.[3]

—And does the Count de B****, said I, read Shakespear? *C'est un Esprit fort;*[4] replied the bookseller.—He loves English books; and what is more to his honour, Monsieur, he loves the English too. You speak this so civilly, said I, that 'tis enough to oblige an Englishman to lay out a Louis d'or or two at your shop—the bookseller made a bow, and was going to say something, when a young decent girl of about twenty, who by her air and dress, seemed to be *fille de chambre* to some devout woman of fashion, came into the shop and asked for *Les Egarments du Cœur & de l'Esprit:*[5] the bookseller gave her the book directly; she pulled out a little green sattin purse run round with a ribband of the same colour, and putting her finger and thumb into it, she took out the money, and paid for it. As I had nothing more to stay me in the shop, we both walked out at the door together.

—— And what have you to do, my dear, said I, with *The Wanderings of the Heart*, who scarce know yet you have one? nor till love has first told you it, or some faithless shepherd has made it ache, can'st thou ever be sure it is so.—*Le Dieu m'en guard!*[6] said the girl.—With reason, said I—for if it is a good one, 'tis pity it should be stolen: 'tis a little treasure to thee, and gives a better air to your face, than if it was dress'd out with pearls.

Crébillon fils .63

The young girl listened with a submissive attention, holding her sattin purse by its ribband in her hand all the time—'Tis a very small one, said I, taking hold of the bottom of it—she held it towards me—and there is very little in it, my dear, said I; but be but as good as thou art handsome, and heaven will fill it: I had a parcel of crowns in my hand to pay for Shakespear; and as she had let go the purse intirely, I put a single one in; and tying up the ribband in a bow-knot, returned it to her.

The young girl made me more a humble courtesy than a low one—'twas one of those quiet, thankful sinkings where the spirit bows itself down—the body does no more than tell it. I never gave a girl a crown in my life which gave me half the pleasure.

My advice, my dear, would not have been worth a pin to you, said I, if I had not given this along with it: but now, when you see the crown, you'll remember it—so don't, my dear, lay it out in ribbands.

Upon my word, Sir, said the girl, earnestly, I am incapable—in saying which, as is usual in little bargains of honour, she gave me her hand—*En verite, Monsieur, je mettrai cet argent apart*,[7] said she.

When a virtuous convention is made betwixt man and woman, it sanctifies their most private walks: so notwithstanding it was dusky, yet as both our roads lay the same way, we made no scruple of walking along the Quai de Conti together.

She made me a second courtesy in setting off, and before we got twenty yards from the door, as if she had not done enough before, she made a sort of a little stop to tell me again,—she thank'd me.

It was a small tribute, I told her, which I could not avoid paying to virtue, and would not be mistaken in the person I had been rendering it to for the world—but I see innocence, my dear, in your face—and foul befal the man who ever lays a snare in its way!

The girl seem'd affected some way or other with what I said—she gave a low sigh—I found I was not impowered to enquire at all after it—so said nothing more till I got to the corner of the Rue de Nevers, where we were to part.

—But is this the way, my dear, said I, to the hotel de Modene? she told me it was—or, that I might go by the Rue de Guineygaude, which was the next turn.—Then I'll go, my dear, by the Rue de Guineygaude, said I, for two reasons; first I shall please myself, and next I shall give you the protection of my company as far on your way as I can. The girl was sensible I was civil—and said, she wish'd the hotel de Modene was in the Rue de St. Pierre—— You live there? said I.—She told me she was *fille de chambre* to Madame R****—Good God! said I, 'tis the very lady for whom I have brought a letter from Amiens—The girl told me that Madame R****, she believed expected a stranger with a letter, and was impatient to see him—so I desired the girl to present my compliments to Madame R****, and say I would certainly wait upon her in the morning.

We stood still at the corner of the Rue de Nevers whilst this pass'd— We then stopp'd a moment whilst she disposed of her *Egarments de Cœur*, &c. more commodiously than carrying them in her hand—they were two volumes; so I held the second for her whilst she put the first into her pocket; and then she held her pocket, and I put in the other after it.

'Tis sweet to feel by what fine-spun threads our affections are drawn together.

We set off a-fresh, and as she took her third step, the girl put her hand within my arm—I was just bidding her—but she did it of herself with that undeliberating simplicity, which shew'd it was out of her head that she had never seen me before. For my own part, I felt the conviction of consanguinity so strongly, that I could not help turning half round to look in her face, and see if I could trace out any thing in it of a family likeness—Tut! said I, are we not all relations?

When we arrived at the turning up of the Rue de Guineygaude, I stopp'd to bid her adieu for good an all: the girl would thank me again for my company and kindness—She bid me adieu twice—I repeated it as often; and so cordial was the parting between us, that had it happen'd any where else, I'm not sure but I should have signed it with a kiss of charity, as warm and holy as an apostle.

But in Paris, as none kiss each other but the men—I did, what amounted to the same thing——
——I bid God bless her.

65

THE PASSPORT.
PARIS.

W HEN I got home to my hotel, La Fleur told me I had been enquired after by the Lieutenant de Police—The duce take it! said I——I know the reason. It is time the reader should know it, for in the order of things in which it happened, it was omitted; not that it was out of my head; but that had I told it then, it might have been forgot now—and now is the time I want it.

I had left London with so much precipitation, that it never enter'd my mind that we were at war with France;[8] and had reach'd Dover, and look'd through my glass at the hills beyond Boulogne, before the idea presented itself; and with this in its train, that there was no getting there without a passport. Go but to the end of a street, I have a mortal aversion for returning back no wiser than I set out; and as this was one of the greatest efforts I had ever made for knowledge, I could less bear the thoughts of it: so hearing the Count de **** had hired the packet, I begg'd he would take me in his *suite*. The Count had some little knowledge of me, so made little or no difficulty—only said, his incli-nation to serve me could reach no further than Calais; as he was to return by way of Brussels to Paris: however, when I had once pass'd there, I might get to Paris without interruption; but that in Paris I must make friends and shift for myself.—Let me get to Paris, Monsieur le Count, said I—and I shall do very well. So I embark'd, and never thought more of the matter.

When La Fleur told me the Lieutenant de Police had been enquiring after me—the thing instantly recurred—and by the time La Fleur had well told me, the master of the hotel came into my room to tell me the same thing, with this addition to it, that my passport had been particularly ask'd after: the master of the hotel concluded with saying, He hoped I had one.—Not I, faith! said I.

The master of the hotel retired three steps from me, as from an infected person, as I declared this—and poor La Fleur advanced three steps towards me, and with that sort of movement which a good soul makes to succour a distress'd one—the fellow won my heart by it; and from that single *trait*, I knew his character as perfectly, and could rely upon it as firmly, as if he had served me with fidelity for seven years.

Mon seignior! cried the master of the hotel—but recollecting himself as he made the exclamation, he instantly changed the tone of it—If Monsieur, said he, has not a passport (*apparament*) in all likelihood he has friends in Paris who can procure him one.—Not that I know of, quoth I, with an air of indifference.—Then *certes*, replied he, you'll be sent to the Bastile or the Chatelet, *au moins*. Poo! said I, the king of France is a good natured soul—he'll hurt no body.—*Cela n'empeche pas*,[9] said he—you will certainly be sent to the Bastile to-morrow morning.—But I've taken your lodgings for a month, answer'd I, and I'll not quit them a day before the time for all the kings of France in the world. La Fleur whisper'd in my ear, That no body could oppose the king of France.

Pardi! said my host, *ces Messieurs Anglois sont des gens tres extraordinaires*[10]—and having both said and sworn it—he went out.

THE PASSPORT.
The Hotel at Paris.

I COULD not find in my heart to torture La Fleur's with a serious look upon the subject of my embarrassment, which was the reason I had treated it so cavalierly: and to shew him how light it lay upon my mind, I dropt the subject entirely; and whilst he waited upon me at supper, talk'd to him with more than usual gaiety about Paris, and of the opera comique.—La Fleur had been there himself, and had followed me through the streets as far as the bookseller's shop; but seeing me come out with the young *fille de chambre*, and that we walk'd down the Quai de Conti together, La Fleur deem'd it unnecessary to follow me a step further—so making his own reflections upon it, he took a shorter cut——— and got to the hotel in time to be inform'd of the affair of the Police against my arrival.

As soon as the honest creature had taken away, and gone down to sup himself, I then began to think a little seriously about my situation.—

—And here, I know, Eugenius, thou wilt smile at the remembrance of a short dialogue which pass'd betwixt us the moment I was going to set out——— I must tell it here.

Eugenius, knowing that I was as little subject to be overburthen'd with money as thought, had drawn me aside to interrogate me how much I had taken care for; upon telling him the exact sum, Eugenius shook his head, and said it would not do; so pull'd out his purse in order to empty it into mine.—I've enough in conscience, Eugenius, said I. ——— Indeed, Yorick, you have not, replied Eugenius—I know France and Italy better than you. ——— But you don't consider, Eugenius, said I, refusing his offer, that before I have been three days in Paris, I shall take care to say or do something or other for which I shall get clapp'd up into the Bastile, and that I shall live there a couple of months entirely at the king of France's expence.—I beg pardon, said Eugenius, drily: really, I had forgot that resource.

Now the event I treated gaily came seriously to my door.

Is it folly, or nonchalance, or philosophy, or pertinacity—or what is it in me, that, after all, when La Fleur had gone down stairs, and I was quite alone, that I could not bring down my mind to think of it otherwise than I had then spoken of it to Eugenius?

—And as for the Bastile! the terror is in the word—Make the most of it you can, said I to myself, the Bastile is but another word for a tower—and a tower is but another word for a house you can't get out of—Mercy on the gouty! for they are in it twice a year—but with nine livres a day, and pen and ink and paper and patience, albeit a man can't get out, he may do very well within—at least for a month or six weeks; at the end of which, if he is a harmless fellow his innocence appears, and he comes out a better and wiser man than he went in.

I had some occasion (I forget what) to step into the court-yard, as I settled this account; and remember I walk'd down stairs in no small triumph with the conceit of my reasoning—Beshrew the *sombre* pencil!

said I vauntingly—for I envy not its powers, which paints the evils of life with so hard and deadly a colouring. The mind sits terrified at the objects she has magnified herself, and blackened: reduce them to their proper size and hue she overlooks them—'Tis true, said I, correcting the proposition—the Bastile is not an evil to be despised—but strip it of its towers—fill up the fossè—unbarricade the doors—call it simply a confinement, and suppose 'tis some tyrant of a distemper—and not of a man which holds you in it—the evil half vanishes, and you bear the other half without complaint.

I was interrupted in the hey-day of this soliloquy, with a voice which I took to be of a child, which complained "it could not get out."—I look'd up and down the passage, and seeing neither man, woman, or child, I went out without further attention.

In my return back through the passage, I heard the same words repeated twice over; and looking up, I saw it was a starling hung in a little cage.—"I can't get out—I can't get out," said the starling.

I stood looking at the bird: and to every person who came through the passage it ran fluttering to the side towards which they approach'd it, with the same lamentation of its captivity—"I can't get out," said the starling—God help thee! said I, but I'll let thee out, cost what it will; so I turn'd about the cage to get to the door; it was twisted and double twisted so fast with wire, there was no getting it open without pulling the cage to pieces—I took both hands to it.

The bird flew to the place where I was attempting his deliverance, and thrusting his head through the trellis, press'd his breast against it, as if impatient—I fear, poor creature! said I, I cannot set thee at liberty—"No," said the starling—"I can't get out—I can't get out," said the starling.

I vow, I never had my affections more tenderly awakened; nor do I remember an incident in my life, where the dissipated spirits, to which my reason had been a bubble, were so suddenly call'd home. Mechanical as the notes were, yet so true in tune to nature were they chanted, that in one moment they overthrew all my systematic reasonings upon the Bastile; and I heavily walk'd up stairs, unsaying every word I had said in going down them.

Disguise thyself as thou wilt, still slavery! said I—still thou art a bitter draught; and though thousands in all ages have been made to drink of thee, thou art no less bitter on that account.[11]—'tis thou, thrice sweet and gracious goddess, addressing myself to LIBERTY, whom all in public or in private worship, whose taste is grateful, and ever wilt be so, till NATURE herself shall change—no *tint* of words can spot thy snowy mantle, or chymic[12] power turn thy sceptre into iron—with thee to smile upon him as he eats his crust, the swain is happier than his monarch, from whose court thou art exiled—Gracious heaven! cried I, kneeling down upon the last step but one in my ascent—grant me but health, thou great Bestower of it, and give me but this fair goddess as my companion—and shower down thy mitres, if it seems good unto thy divine providence, upon those heads which are aching for them.

THE CAPTIVE.
PARIS.

T HE bird in his cage pursued me into my room; I sat down close to my table, and leaning my head upon my hand, I begun to figure to myself the miseries of confinement. I was in a right frame for it, and so I gave full scope to my imagination.

I was going to begin with the millions of my fellow creatures born to no inheritance but slavery;[13] but finding, however affecting the picture was, that I could not bring it near me, and that the multitude of sad groups in it did but distract me.—

—I took a single captive, and having first shut him up in his dungeon, I then look'd through the twilight of his grated door to take his picture.

I beheld his body half wasted away with long expectation and confinement, and felt what kind of sickness of the heart it was which arises from hope deferr'd.[14] Upon looking nearer I saw him pale and feverish: in thirty years the western breeze had not once fann'd his blood—he had seen no sun, no moon in all that time—nor had the voice of friend or kinsman breathed through his lattice—his children—

—But here my heart began to bleed—and I was forced to go on with another part of the portrait.

He was sitting upon the ground upon a little straw, in the furthest corner of his dungeon, which was alternately his chair and bed: a little calender of small sticks were laid at the head notch'd all over with the dismal days and nights he had pass'd there—he had one of these little sticks in his hand, and with a rusty nail he was etching another day of misery to add to the heap. As I darkened the little light he had, he lifted up a hopeless eye towards the door, then cast it down—shook his head, and went on with his work of affliction. I heard his chains upon his legs, as he turn'd his body to lay his little stick upon the bundle—He gave a deep sigh—I saw the iron enter into his soul[15]— I burst into tears—I could not sustain the picture of confinement which my fancy had drawn—I startled up from my chair, and calling La Fleur, I bid him bespeak me a *remise*, and have it ready at the door of the hotel by nine in the morning.

—I'll go directly, said I, myself to Monsieur Le Duke de Choiseul.[16]

La Fleur would have put me to bed; but not willing he should see any thing upon my cheek, which would cost the honest fellow a heart ache—I told him I would go to bed by myself—and bid him go do the same.

THE STARLING.
ROAD TO VERSAILLES.

I GOT into my *remise* the hour I proposed: La Fleur got up behind, and I bid the coachman make the best of his way to Versailles.

As there was nothing in this road, or rather nothing which I look for in travelling, I cannot fill up the blank better than with a short history of this self-same bird, which became the subject of the last chapter.

Whilst the Honourable Mr. **** was waiting for a wind at Dover it had been caught upon the cliffs before it could well fly, by an English lad who was his groom; who not caring to destroy it, had taken it in his breast into the packet—and by course of feeding it, and taking it once under his protection, in a day or two grew fond of it, and got it safe along with him to Paris.

At Paris the lad had laid out a livre in a little cage for the starling, and as he had little to do better the five months his master stay'd there, he taught it in his mother's tongue the four simple words—(and no more)—to which I own'd myself so much its debtor.

Upon his master's going on for Italy—the lad had given it to the master of the hotel—But his little song for liberty, being in an *unknown* language at Paris—the bird had little or no store set by him—so La Fleur bought both him and his cage for me for a bottle of Burgundy.

In my return from Italy I brought him with me to the country in whose language he had learn'd his notes—and telling the story of him to Lord A—Lord A begg'd the bird of me—in a week Lord A gave him to Lord B—Lord B made a present of him to Lord C—and Lord C's gentleman sold him to Lord D's for a shilling—Lord D gave him to Lord E—and so on—half round the alphabet—From that rank he pass'd into the lower house, and pass'd the hands of as many commoners —— But as all these wanted to *get in*—and my bird wanted to get out—he had almost as little store set by him in London as in Paris.

It is impossible but many of my readers must have heard of him; and if any by mere chance have ever seen him—I beg leave to inform them, that that bird was my bird—or some vile copy set up to represent him.

I have nothing further to add upon him, but that from that time to this, I have borne this poor starling as the crest to my arms.[17]—Thus:

——And let the heralds officers twist his neck about if they dare.

THE ADDRESS.
VERSAILLES.

I SHOULD not like to have my enemy take a view of my mind, when I am going to ask protection of any man: for which reason I generally endeavour to protect myself; but this going to Monsieur Le Duc de C***** was an act of compulsion—had it been an act of choice, I should have done it, I suppose, like other people.

How many mean plans of dirty address, as I went along, did my servile heart form! I deserved the Bastile for every one of them.

Then nothing would serve me, when I got within sight of Versailles, but putting words and sentences together, and conceiving attitudes and tones to wreath myself into Monsieur Le Duc de C*****'s good graces—This will do—— said I—Just as well, retorted I again, as a coat carried up to him by an adventurous taylor, without taking his measure—Fool! continued I—see Monsieur Le Duc's face first— observe what character is written in it; take notice in what posture he stands to hear you—mark the turns and expressions of his body and limbs—And for the tone—the first sound which comes from his lips will give it you; and from all these together you'll compound an address at once upon the spot, which cannot disgust the Duke—the ingredients are his own, and most likely to go down.

Well! said I, I wish it well over—Coward again! as if man to man was not equal, throughout the whole surface of the globe; and if in the field—why not face to face in the cabinet too? And trust me, Yorick, whenever it is not so, man is false to himself; and betrays his own succours[18] ten times, where nature does it once. Go to the Duc de C**** with the Bastile in thy looks—My life for it, thou wilt be sent back to Paris in half an hour, with an escort.

I believe so, said I—Then I'll go to the Duke, by heaven! with all the gaity and debonairness in the world.—

—And there you are wrong again, replied I—A heart at ease, Yorick, flies into no extremes—'tis ever on its center.—Well! well!

cried I, as the coachman turn'd in at the gates—I find I shall do very well: and by the time he had wheel'd round the court, and brought me up to the door, I found myself so much the better for my own lecture, that I neither ascended the steps like a victim to justice, who was to part with life upon the topmost,—nor did I mount them with a skip and a couple of strides, as I do when I fly up, Eliza! to thee, to meet it.

As I enter'd the door of the saloon, I was met by a person who possibly might be the maitre d'hotel, but had more the air of one of the under secretaries, who told me the Duc de C**** was busy—I am utterly ignorant, said I, of the forms of obtaining an audience, being an absolute stranger, and what is worse in the present conjuncture of affairs, being an Englishman too. —— He replied, that did not increase the difficulty.—I made him a slight bow, and told him, I had something of importance to say to Monsieur Le Duc. The secretary look'd towards the stairs, as if he was about to leave me to carry up this account to some one—But I must not mislead you, said I—for what I have to say is of no manner of importance to Monsieur Le Duc de C****—but of great importance to myself.—*C'est une autre affaire*,[19] replied he —— Not at all, said I, to a man of gallantry.—But pray, good sir, continued I, when can a stranger hope to have *accesse*? In not less than two hours, said he, looking at his watch. The number of equipages in the court-yard seem'd to justify the calculation, that I could have no nearer a prospect—and as walking backwards and forwards in the saloon, without a soul to commune with, was for the time as bad as being in the Bastile itself, I instantly went back to my *remise*, and bid the coachman drive me to the *cordon bleu*, which was the nearest hotel.

I think there is a fatality in it—I seldom go to the place I set out for.

LE PATISSER.[20]
VERSAILLES.

BEFORE I had got half-way down the street, I changed my mind: as I am at Versailles, thought I, I might as well take a view of the town; so I pull'd the cord, and ordered the coachman to drive round some of the principal streets—I suppose the town is not very large, said I.—The coachman begg'd pardon for setting me right, and told me it was very superb, and that numbers of the first dukes and marquises and counts had hotels—The Count de B****, of whom the bookseller at the Quai de Conti had spoke so handsomely the night before, came instantly into my mind.—And why should I not go, thought I, to the Count de B****, who has so high an idea of English books, and Englishmen—and tell him my story? so I changed my mind a second time—In truth it was the third; for I had intended that day for Madame de R**** in the Rue St. Pierre, and had devoutly sent her word by her *fille de chambre* that I would assuredly wait upon her—but I am govern'd by circumstances—I cannot govern them: so seeing a man standing with a basket on the other side of the street, as if he had something to sell, I bid La Fleur go up to him and enquire for the Count's hotel.

La Fleur return'd a little pale; and told me it was a Chevalier de St. Louis selling *patès*[21]—It is impossible, La Fleur! said I.—La Fleur could no more account for the phenomenon than myself; but persisted in his story: he had seen the croix set in gold, with its red ribband, he said, tied to his button-hole—and had look'd into the basket and seen the *patès* which the Chevalier was selling; so could not be mistaken in that.

Such a reverse in man's life awakens a better principle than curiosity: I could not help looking for some time at him as I sat in the *remise*—the more I look'd at him—his croix and his basket, the stronger they wove themselves into my brain—I got out of the *remise* and went towards him.

He was begirt with a clean linen apron which fell below his knees, and with a sort of a bib went half way up his breast; upon the top of this, but a little below the hem, hung his croix. His basket of little *patès* was cover'd over with a white damask napkin; another of the same kind was spread at the bottom; and there was a look of *propreté*[22] and neatness throughout; that one might have bought his *patès* of him, as much from appetite as sentiment.

He made an offer of them to neither; but stood still with them at the corner of a hotel, for those to buy who chose it, without solicitation.

He was about forty-eight—of a sedate look, something approaching to gravity. I did not wonder.—I went up rather to the basket than him, and having lifted up the napkin and taken one of his *patès* into my hand—I begg'd he would explain the appearance which affected me.

He told me in a few words, that the best part of his life had pass'd in the service, in which, after spending a small patrimony, he had obtain'd a company and the croix with it; but that at the conclusion of the last peace,[23] his regiment being reformed, and the whole corps, with those of some other regiments, left without any provision—he found himself in a wide world without friends, without a livre—and indeed, said he, without any thing but this—(pointing, as he said it, to his croix)—The poor chevalier won my pity, and he finish'd the scene, with winning my esteem too.

The king, he said, was the most generous of princes, but his generosity could neither relieve or reward every one, and it was only his misfortune to be amongst the number. He had a little wife, he said, whom he loved, who did the *patisserie*; and added, he felt no dishonour in defending her and himself from want in this way—unless Providence had offer'd him a better.

It would be wicked to with-hold a pleasure from the good, in passing over what happen'd to this poor Chevalier of St. Louis about nine months after.

It seems he usually took his stand near the iron gates which lead up to the palace, and as his croix had caught the eye of numbers, numbers had made the same enquiry which I had done—He had told them the same story, and always with so much modesty and good sense, that it had reach'd at last the king's ears—who hearing the Chevalier had been a gallant officer, and respected by the whole regiment as a man of honour and integrity—he broke up his little trade by a pension of fifteen hundred livres a year.

As I have told this to please the reader, I beg he will allow me to relate another out of its order, to please myself—the two stories reflect light upon each other,—and 'tis a pity they should be parted.

THE SWORD.
RENNES.

W HEN states and empires have their periods of declension, and feel in their turns what distress and poverty is—I stop not to tell the causes which gradually brought the house d'E**** in Britany into decay. The Marquis d'E**** had fought up against his condition with great firmness; wishing to preserve, and still shew to the world some little fragments of what his ancestors had been—their indiscretions had put it out of his power. There was enough left for the little exigencies of *obscurity*—But he had two boys who look'd up to him for *light*—he thought they deserved it. He had tried his sword—it could not open the way—the *mounting*[24] was too expensive—and simple œconomy was not a match for it—there was no resource but commerce.

In any other province in France, save Britany, this was smiting the root for ever of the little tree his pride and affection wish'd to see re-blossom—But in Britany, there being a provision for this, he avail'd himself of it; and taking an occasion when the states were assembled at Rennes,[25] the Marquis, attended with his two boys, enter'd the court; and having pleaded the right of an ancient law of the duchy, which, though seldom claim'd, he said, was no less in force; he took his sword from his side—Here—said he—take it; and be trusty guardians of it, till better times put me in condition to reclaim it.

The president accepted the Marquis's sword—he stay'd a few minutes to see it deposited in the archives of his house—and departed.

The Marquis and his whole family embarked the next day for Martinico, and in about nineteen or twenty years of successful application to business, with some unlook'd for bequests from distant branches of his house—return'd home to reclaim his nobility and to support it.

It was an incident of good fortune which will never happen to any traveller, but a sentimental one, that I should be at Rennes at the very time of this solemn requisition: I call it solemn—it was so to me.

The Marquis enter'd the court with his whole family: he supported his lady—his eldest son supported his sister, and his youngest was at the other extreme of the line next his mother.—he put his handkerchief to his face twice—

—There was a dead silence. When the Marquis had approach'd within six paces of the tribunal, he gave the Marchioness to his youngest son, and advancing three steps before his family—he reclaim'd his sword. His sword was given him, and the moment he got it into his hand he drew it almost out of the scabbard—'twas the shining face of a friend he had once given up—he look'd attentively along it, beginning at the hilt, as if to see whether it was the same—when observing a little rust which it had contracted near the point, he brought it near his eye, and bending his head down over it—I think I saw a tear fall upon the place: I could not be deceived by what followed.

"I shall find, said he, some *other way*, to get it off."

When the Marquis had said this, he return'd his sword into its scabbard, made a bow to the guardians of it—and, with his wife and daughter and his two sons following him, walk'd out.

O how I envied him his feelings!

THE PASSPORT.
VERSAILLES.

I FOUND no difficulty in getting admittance to Monsieur Le Count de B****. The set of Shakespears was laid upon the table, and he was tumbling them over.[26] I walk'd up close to the table, and giving first such a look at the books as to make him conceive I knew what they were—I told him I had come without any one to present me, knowing I should meet with a friend in his apartment who, I trusted, would do it for me—it is my countryman the great Shakespear, said I, pointing to his works—*et ayez la bontè, mon cher ami*, apostrophizing his spirit, added I, *de me faire cet honneur la.*——[27]

The Count smil'd at the singularity of the introduction; and seeing I look'd a little pale and sickly, insisted upon my taking an arm-chair: so I sat down; and to save him conjectures upon a visit so out of all rule, I told him simply of the incident in the bookseller's shop, and how that had impell'd me rather to go to him with the story of a little embarrassment I was under, than to any other man in France—And what is your embarrassment? let me hear it, said the Count. So I told him the story just as I have told it the reader—

—And the master of my hotel, said I, as I concluded it, will needs have it, Monsieur le Count, that I shall be sent to the Bastile—but I have no apprehensions, continued I—for in falling into the hands of the most polish'd people in the world, and being conscious I was a true man, and not come to spy the nakedness of the land,[28] I scarce thought I laid at their mercy.—It does not suit the gallantry of the French, Monsieur le Count, said I, to shew it against invalids.

An animated blush came into the Count de B****'s cheeks, as I spoke this—*Ne craignez rien*[29]—Don't fear, said he—Indeed I don't, replied I again—besides, continued I a little sportingly—I have come laughing all the way from London to Paris, and I do not think Monsieur le Duc de Choiseul is such an enemy to mirth, as to send me back crying for my pains.

—— My application to you, Monsieur le Compte de B**** (making him a low bow) is to desire he will not.

The Count heard me with great good nature, or I had not said half as much—and once or twice said—*C'est bien dit*.[30] So I rested my cause there—and determined to say no more about it.

The Count led the discourse: we talk'd of indifferent things;—of books and politicks, and men—and then of women—God bless them all! said I, after much discourse about them—there is not a man upon earth who loves them so much as I do: after all the foibles I have seen, and all the satires I have read against them, still I love them; being firmly persuaded that a man who has not a sort of an affection for the whole sex, is incapable of ever loving a single one as he ought.

Hèh bien! Monsieur l'Anglois, said the Count, gaily—You are not come to spy the nakedness of the land—I believe you—*ni encore*,[31] I dare say, *that* of our women—But permit me to conjecture—if, *par hazard*, they fell in your way—that the prospect would not affect you.

I have something within me which cannot bear the shock of the least indecent insinuation: in the sportability of chit-chat I have often endeavoured to conquer it, and with infinite pain have hazarded a thousand things to a dozen of the sex together—the least of which I could not venture to a single one, to gain heaven.

Excuse me, Monsieur Le Count, said I—as for the nakedness of your land, if I saw it, I should cast my eyes over it with tears in them—and for that of your women (blushing at the idea he had excited in me) I am so evangelical in this, and have such a fellow-feeling for what ever is *weak* about them, that I would cover it with a garment, if I knew how to throw it on—But I could wish, continued I, to spy the *nakedness* of their hearts, and through the different disguises of customs, climates, and religion, find out what is good in them, to fashion my own by—and therefore am I come.[32]

It is for this reason, Monsieur le Compte, continued I, that I have not seen the Palais royal—nor the Luxembourg—nor the Façade of the Louvre[33]—nor have attempted to swell the catalogues we have of pictures, statues, and churches—I conceive every fair being as a temple, and would rather enter in,[34] and see the original drawings and loose sketches hung up in it, than the transfiguration of Raphael itself.[35]

The thirst of this, continued I, as impatient as that which inflames the breast of the connoisseur, has led me from my own home into France—and from France will lead me through Italy—'tis a quiet journey of the heart in pursuit of NATURE, and those affections which rise out of her, which make us love each other—and the world, better than we do.[36]

The Count said a great many civil things to me upon the occasion; and added very politely how much he stood obliged to Shakespear for making me known to him—but, *a-propos*, said he—Shakespear is full of great things—He forgot a small punctillio of announcing your name—it puts you under a necessity of doing it yourself.

THE PASSPORT.
VERSAILLES.

THERE is not a more perplexing affair in life to me, than to set about telling any one who I am[37]—for there is scarce any body I cannot give a better account of than of myself; and I have often wish'd I could do it in a single word—and have an end of it. It was the only time and occasion in my life, I could accomplish this to any purpose— for Shakespear lying upon the table, and recollecting I was in his books, I took up Hamlet, and turning immediately to the grave-diggers scene in the fifth act, I lay'd my finger upon YORICK, and advancing the book to the Count, with my finger all the way over the name—Me, *Voici!* said I.

Now whether the idea of poor Yorick's skull was put out of the Count's mind, by the reality of my own, or by what magic he could drop a period of seven or eight hundred years, makes nothing in this account—'tis certain the French conceive better than they combine— I wonder at nothing in this world, and the less at this; inasmuch as one of the first of our own church, for whose candour and paternal sentiments I have the highest veneration, fell into the same mistake in the very same case.—"He could not bear, he said, to look into sermons wrote by the king of Denmark's jester."[38]—Good, my lord! said I—but there are two Yoricks. The Yorick your lordship thinks of, has been dead and buried eight hundred years ago; he flourish'd in Horwendillus's court—the other Yorick is myself, who have flourish'd my lord in no court—He shook his head—Good God! said I, you might as well confound Alexander the Great, with Alexander the Copper-smith, my lord —— 'Twas all one, he replied—[39]

—If Alexander king of Macedon could have translated your lordship, said I—I'm sure your Lordship would not have said so.

The poor Count de B**** fell but into the same *error*—

—— *Et, Monsieur, est il Yorick?* cried the Count.—*Je le suis*, said I.— *Vous?—Moi—moi qui ai l'honneur de vous parler, Monsieur le Compte— Mon Dieu!* said he, embracing me —— *Vous etes Yorick.*[40]

The Count instantly put the Shakespear into his pocket—and left me alone in his room.

THE PASSPORT.
VERSAILLES.

I COULD not conceive why the Count de B**** had gone so abruptly out of the room, any more than I could conceive why he had put the Shakespear into his pocket—*Mysteries which must explain themselves, are not worth the loss of time, which a conjecture about them takes up:* 'twas better to read Shakespear; so taking up, "*Much Ado about Nothing*," I transported myself instantly from the chair I sat in to Messina in Sicily, and got so busy with Don Pedro and Benedick and Beatrice, that I thought not of Versailles, the Count, or the Passport.

Sweet pliability of man's spirit, that can at once surrender itself to illusions, which cheat expectation and sorrow of their weary moments!——long—long since had ye number'd out my days, had I not trod so great a part of them upon this enchanted ground: when my way is too rough for my feet, or too steep for my strength, I get off it, to some smooth velvet path which fancy has scattered over with rose-buds of delights; and having taken a few turns in it, come back strengthen'd and refresh'd—When evils press sore upon me, and there is no retreat from them in this world, then I take a new course—I leave it—and as I have a clearer idea of the elysian fields than I have of heaven, I force myself, like Eneas, into them—I see him meet the pensive shade of his forsaken Dido—and wish to recognize it—I see the injured spirit wave her head, and turn off silent from the author of her miseries and dishonours[41]—I lose the feelings for myself in hers— and in those affections which were wont to make me mourn for her when I was at school.

Surely this is not walking in a vain shadow—nor does man disquiet himself in vain,[42] *by it*—he oftener does so in trusting the issue of his commotions to reason only.—I can safely say for myself, I was never able to conquer any one single bad sensation in my heart so decisively, as by beating up as fast as I could for some kindly and gentle sensation, to fight it upon its own ground.

When I had got to the end of the third act, the Count de B**** entered with my Passport in his hand. Mons. le Duc de C****, said the Count, is as good a prophet, I dare say, as he is a statesman— *Un homme qui rit*, said the duke, *ne sera jamais dangereuz.*—Had it been for any one but the king's jester, added the Count, I could not have got it these two hours.—*Pardonnez moi*, Mons. Le Compte, said I—I am not the king's jester.—But you are Yorick?—Yes.—*Et vous plaisantez?*[43]—I answered, Indeed I did jest—but was not paid for it—'twas entirely at my own expence.

We have no jester at court, Mons. Le Compte, said I, the last we had was in the licentious reign of Charles the IId[44]—since which time our manners have been so gradually refining, that our court at present is so full of patriots,[45] who wish for *nothing* but the honours and wealth of their country—and our ladies are all so chaste, so spotless, so good, so devout—there is nothing for a jester to make a jest of—

Voila un persiflage![46] cried the Count.

THE PASSPORT.
VERSAILLES.

AS the Passport was directed to all lieutenant governors, governors, and commandants of cities, generals of armies, justiciaries, and all officers of justice, to let Mr. Yorick, the king's jester, and his baggage, travel quietly along—I own the triumph of obtaining the Passport was not a little tarnish'd by the figure I cut in it—But there is nothing unmixt in this world; and some of the gravest of our divines have carried it so far as to affirm, that enjoyment itself was attended even with a sigh—and that the greatest *they knew of*, terminated *in a general way*, in little better than a convulsion.

I remember the grave and learned Bevoriskius,[47] in his commentary upon the generations from Adam, very naturally breaks off in the middle of a note to give an account to the world of a couple of sparrows upon the out-edge of his window, which had incommoded him all the time he wrote, and at last had entirely taken him off from his genealogy.

—'Tis strange! writes Bevoriskius; but the facts are certain, for I have had the curiosity to mark them down one by one with my pen—but the cock-sparrow during the little time that I could have finished the other half this note, has actually interrupted me with the reiteration of his caresses three and twenty times and a half.

How merciful, adds Bevoriskius, is heaven to his creatures!

Ill fated Yorick! that the gravest of thy brethren should be able to write that to the world, which stains thy face with crimson, to copy in even thy study.

But this is nothing to my travels—So I twice—twice beg pardon for it.

CHARACTER.
VERSAILLES.

AND how do you find the French? said the Count de B****, after he had given me the Passport.

The reader may suppose that after so obliging a proof of courtesy, I could not be at a loss to say something handsome to the enquiry.

—*Mais passe, pour cela*—Speak frankly, said he; do you find all the urbanity in the French which the world give us the honour of?—I had found every thing, I said, which confirmed it—*Vraiment*, said the count.—*Les François sont polis* [48]—To an excess, replied I.

The count took notice of the word *excesse*; and would have it I meant more than I said. I defended myself a long time as well as I could against it—he insisted I had a reserve, and that I would speak my opinion frankly.

I believe, Mons. Le Compte, said I, that man has a certain compass, as well as an instrument; and that the social and other calls have occasion by turns for every key in him; so that if you begin a note too high or too low, there must be a want either in the upper or under part, to fill up the system of harmony.—The Count de B**** did not understand music, so desired me to explain it some other way. A polish'd nation, my dear Count, said I, makes every one its debtor; and besides urbanity itself, like the fair sex, has so many charms; it goes against the heart to say it can do ill; and yet, I believe, there is but a certain line of perfection, that man, take him altogether, is empower'd to arrive at—if he gets beyond, he rather exchanges qualities, than gets them. I must not presume to say, how far this has affected the French in the subject we are speaking of— but should it ever be the case of the English, in the progress of their refinements, to arrive at the same polish which distinguishes the French, if we did not lose the *politesse de cœur*,[49] which inclines men more to human actions, than courteous ones—we should at least lose that distinct variety and originality of character, which distinguishes them, not only from each other, but from all the world besides.

I had a few king William's shillings as smooth as glass in my pocket; and foreseeing they would be of use in the illustration of my hypothesis, I had got them into my hand, when I had proceeded so far—

See, Mons. Le Compte, said I, rising up, and laying them before him upon the table—by jingling and rubbing one against another for seventy years together in one body's pocket or another's, they are become so much alike, you can scarce distinguish one shilling from another.

The English, like antient medals, kept more apart, and passing but few peoples hands, preserve the first sharpnesses which the fine hand of nature has given them—they are not so pleasant to feel—but in return, the legend is so visible, that at the first look you see whose image and superscription they bear.—But the French, Mons. Le Compte, added I, wishing to soften what I had said, have so many excellencies, they can the better spare this—they are a loyal, a gallant, a generous, an ingenious, and good temper'd people as is under heaven—if they have a fault—they are too *serious*.[50]

Mon Dieu! cried the Count, rising out of his chair.

Mais vous plaisantez,[51] said he, correcting his exclamation.—I laid my hand upon my breast, and with earnest gravity assured him, it was my most settled opinion.

The Count said he was mortified, he could not stay to hear my reasons, being engaged to go that moment to dine with the Duc de C****.

But if it is not too far to come to Versailles to eat your soup with me, I beg, before you leave France, I may have the pleasure of knowing you retract your opinion—or, in what manner you support it.—But if you do support it, Mons. Anglois, said he, you must do it with all your powers, because you have the whole world against you.—I promised the Count I would do myself the honour of dining with him before I set out for Italy—so took my leave.

THE TEMPTATION.
PARIS.

W HEN I alighted at the hotel, the porter told me a young woman with a band-box[52] had been that moment enquiring for me.—I do not know, said the porter, whether she is gone away or no. I took the key of my chamber of him, and went up stairs; and when I had got within ten steps of the top of the landing before my door, I met her coming easily down.

It was the fair *fille de chambre* I had walked along the Quai de Conti with: Madame de R**** had sent her upon some commissions to a *merchande de modes*[53] within a step or two of the hotel de Modene; and as I had fail'd in waiting upon her, had bid her enquire if I had left Paris; and if so, whether I had not left a letter address'd to her.

As the fair *fille de chambre* was so near my door she turned back, and went into the room with me for a moment or two whilst I wrote a card.

It was a fine still evening in the latter end of the month of May— the crimson window curtains (which were of the same colour of those of the bed) were drawn close—the sun was setting and reflected through them so warm a tint into the fair *fille de chambre*'s face—I thought she blush'd—the idea of it made me blush myself—we were quite alone; and that super-induced a second blush before the first could get off.

There is a sort of a pleasing half guilty blush, where the blood is more in fault than the man—'tis sent impetuous from the heart, and virtue flies after it—not to call it back, but to make the sensation of it more delicious to the nerves—'tis associated.—

But I'll not describe it.—I felt something at first within me which was not in strict unison with the lesson of virtue I had given her the night before—I sought five minutes for a card—I knew I had not one.—I took up a pen—I laid it down again—my hand trembled— the devil was in me.

I know as well as any one, he is an adversary, whom if we resist, he will fly from us—but I seldom resist him at all; from a terror, that though I may conquer, I may still get a hurt in the combat—so I give up the triumph, for security; and instead of thinking to make him fly, I generally fly myself.

The fair *fille de chambre* came close up to the bureau where I was looking for a card—took up first the pen I cast down, then offered to hold me the ink: she offer'd it so sweetly, I was going to accept it—but I durst not—I have nothing, my dear, said I, to write upon.—Write it, said she, simply, upon any thing.—

I was just going to cry out, Then I will write it, fair girl! upon thy lips.— *metaphor*

If I do, said I, I shall perish—so I took her by the hand, and led her to the door, and begg'd she would not forget the lesson I had given her—She said, Indeed she would not—and as she utter'd it with some earnestness, she turned about, and gave me both her hands, closed together, into mine—it was impossible not to compress them in that situation—I wish'd to let them go; and all the time I held them, I kept arguing within myself against it—and still I held them on.—In two minutes I found I had all the battle to fight over again—and I felt my legs and every limb about me tremble at the idea.

The foot of the bed was within a yard and a half of the place where we were standing—I had still hold of her hands—and how it happened I can give no account, but I neither ask'd her—nor drew her—nor did I think of the bed—but so it did happen, we both sat down.

I'll just shew you, said the fair *fille de chambre*, the little purse I have been making to-day to hold your crown. So she put her hand into her right pocket, which was next me, and felt for it for some time—then into the left—"She had lost it."—I never bore expectation more quietly—it was in her right pocket at last—she pulled it out; it was of green taffeta, lined with a little bit of white quilted sattin, and just big enough to hold the crown—she put it into my hand—it was pretty; and I held it ten minutes with the back of my hand resting upon her lap—looking sometimes at the purse, sometimes on one side of it.

A stitch or two had broke out in the gathers of my stock—the fair *fille de chambre*, without saying a word, took out her little hussive,[54] threaded a small needle, and sew'd it up—I foresaw it would hazard the glory of the day; and as she passed her hand in silence across and across my neck in the manœuvre, I felt the laurels shake which fancy had wreath'd about my head.

A strap had given way in her walk, and the buckle of her shoe was just falling off—See, said the *fille de chambre*, holding up her foot—I could not for my soul but fasten the buckle in return, and putting in the strap—and lifting up the other foot with it, when I had done, to see both were right—in doing it too suddenly—it unavoidably threw the fair *fille de chambre* off her center—and then—

THE CONQUEST.

YES —— and then—Ye whose clay-cold heads and luke-warm hearts can argue down or mask your passions—tell me, what trespass is it that man should have them? or how his spirit stands answerable, to the father of spirits, but for his conduct under them?

If nature has so wove her web of kindness, that some threads of love and desire are entangled with the piece—must the whole web be rent in drawing them out?—Whip me such stoics, great governor of nature! said I to myself—Wherever thy providence shall place me for the trials of my virtue—whatever is my danger—whatever is my situation—let me feel the movements which rise out of it, and which belong to me as a man—and if I govern them as a good one—I will trust the issues to thy justice, for thou hast made us—and not we ourselves.[55]

As I finish'd my address, I raised the fair *fille de chambre* up by the hand, and led her out of the room—she stood by me till I lock'd the door and put the key in my pocket—*and then*—the victory being quite decisive—and not till then, I press'd my lips to her cheek, and, taking her by the hand again, led her safe to the gate of the hotel.

THE MYSTERY.
PARIS.

IF a man knows the heart, he will know it was impossible to go back instantly to my chamber—it was touching a cold key with a flat third to it, upon the close of a piece of musick, which had call'd forth my affections—therefore, when I let go the hand of the *fille de chambre*, I remain'd at the gate of the hotel for some time, looking at every one who pass'd by, and forming conjectures upon them, till my attention got fix'd upon a single object which confounded all kind of reasoning upon him.

It was a tall figure of a philosophic serious, adust look, which pass'd and repass'd sedately along the street, making a turn of about sixty paces on each side of the gate of the hotel—the man was about fifty-two—had a small cane under his arm—was dress'd in a dark drab-colour'd coat, waistcoat, and breeches, which seem'd to have seen some years service—they were still clean, and there was a little air of frugal *proprieté* throughout him. By his pulling off his hat, and his attitude of accosting a good many in his way, I saw he was asking charity; so I got a sous or two out of my pocket ready to give him, as he took me in his turn—he pass'd by me without asking any thing—and yet did not go five steps further before he ask'd charity of a little woman—I was much more likely to have given of the two—He had scarce done with the woman, when he pull'd off his hat to another who was coming the same way.—An ancient gentleman came slowly—and, after him, a young smart one—He let them both pass, and ask'd nothing: I stood observing him half an hour, in which time he had made a dozen turns backwards and forwards, and found that he invariably pursued the same plan.

There were two things very singular in this, which set my brain to work, and to no purpose—the first was, why the man should *only* tell his story to the sex—and secondly—what kind of story it was, and what species of eloquence it could be, which soften'd the hearts of the women, which he knew 'twas to no purpose to practise upon the men.

There were two other circumstances which entangled this mystery—the one was, he told every woman what he had to say in her ear, and in a way which had much more the air of a secret than a petition—the other was, it was always successful—he never stopp'd a woman, but she pull'd out her purse, and immediately gave him something.

I could form no system to explain the phenomenon.

I had got a riddle to amuse me for the rest of the evening, so I walk'd up stairs to my chamber.

THE CASE OF CONSCIENCE.
PARIS.

I WAS immediately followed up by the master of the hotel, who came into my room to tell me I must provide lodgings else where. —How so, friend? said I.—He answer'd, I had had a young woman lock'd up with me two hours that evening in my bed-chamber, and 'twas against the rules of his house.—Very well, said I, we'll all part friends then—for the girl is no worse—and I am no worse—and you will be just as I found you. —— It was enough, he said, to overthrow the credit of his hotel.— *Voyez vous, Monsieur,*[56] said he, pointing to the foot of the bed we had been sitting upon.—I own it had something of the appearance of an evidence; but my pride not suffering me to enter into any detail of the case, I exhorted him to let his soul sleep in peace, as I resolved to let mine do that night, and that I would discharge what I owed him at breakfast.

I should not have minded, *Monsieur*, said he, if you had had twenty girls—'Tis a score more, replied I, interrupting him, than I ever reckon'd upon—Provided, added he, it had been but in a morning.— And does the difference of the time of the day at Paris make a difference in the sin?—It made a difference, he said, in the scandal.—I like a good distinction in my heart; and cannot say I was intolerably out of temper with the man.—I own it is necessary, re-assumed the master of the hotel, that a stranger at Paris should have the opportunities presented to him of buying lace and silk stockings and ruffles, *et tout cela*—and 'tis nothing if a woman comes with a band box.——O' my conscience, said I, she had one; but I never look'd into it.—Then, *Monsieur*, said he, has bought nothing.—Not one earthly thing, replied I.—Because, said he, I could recommend one to you who would use you *en conscience.*[57]—But I must see her this night, said I.—He made me a low bow and walk'd down.

Now shall I triumph over this *maitre d'hotel*, cried I—and what then?—Then I shall let him see I know he is a dirty fellow.—And what then?—What then!—I was too near myself to say it was for the sake of others.—I had no good answer left—there was more of spleen than principle in my project, and I was sick of it before the execution.

In a few minutes the Grisset came in with her box of lace—I'll buy nothing however, said I, within myself.

The Grisset would shew me every thing—I was hard to please: she would not seem to see it; she open'd her little magazine, laid all her laces one after another before me—unfolded and folded them up again one by one with the most patient sweetness—I might buy—or not— she would let me have every thing at my own price—the poor creature seem'd anxious to get a penny; and laid herself out to win me, and not so much in a manner which seem'd artful, as in one I felt simple and caressing.

If there is not a fund of honest cullibility[58] in man, so much the worse—my heart relented, and I gave up my second resolution as quietly as the first—Why should I chastise one for the trespass of another? if thou art tributary to this tyrant of an host, thought I, looking up in her face, so much harder is thy bread.

If I had not had more than four *Louis d'ors* in my purse, there was no such thing as rising up and shewing her the door, till I had first laid three of them out in a pair of ruffles.

—The master of the hotel will share the profit with her—no matter —then I have only paid as many a poor soul has *paid* before me for an act he *could* not do, or think of.

THE RIDDLE.
PARIS.

WHEN La Fleur came up to wait upon me at supper, he told me how sorry the master of the hotel was for his affront to me in bidding me change my lodgings.

A man who values a good night's rest will not lay down with enmity in his heart if he can help it—So I bid La Fleur tell the master of the hotel, that I was sorry on my side for the occasion I had given him—and you may tell him, if you will, La Fleur, added I, that if the young woman should call again, I shall not see her.

This was a sacrifice not to him, but myself, having resolved, after so narrow an escape, to run no more risks, but to leave Paris, if it was possible, with all the virtue I enter'd in.

C'est deroger à noblesse,[59] *Monsieur,* said La Fleur, making me a bow down to the ground as he said it—*Et encore*[60] *Monsieur,* said he, may change his sentiments—and if (*par hazard*) he should like to amuse himself—I find no amusement in it, said I, interrupting him—

Mon Dieu! said La Fleur—and took away.

In an hour's time he came to put me to bed, and was more than commonly officious—something hung upon his lips to say to me, or ask me, which he could not get off: I could not conceive what it was; and indeed gave myself little trouble to find it out, as I had another riddle so much more interesting upon my mind, which was that of the man's asking charity before the door of the hotel—I would have given any thing to have got to the bottom of it; and that, not out of curiosity— 'tis so low a principle of enquiry, in general, I would not purchase the gratification of it with a two-sous piece—but a secret, I thought, which so soon and so certainly soften'd the heart of every woman you came near, was a secret at least equal to the philosopher's stone: had I had both the Indies,[61] I would have given up one to have been master of it.

I toss'd and turn'd it almost all night long in my brains to no manner of purpose; and when I awoke in the morning, I found my spirit as much troubled with my *dreams*, as ever the king of Babylon had been with his; and I will not hesitate to affirm, it would have puzzled all the wise men of Paris, as much as those of Chaldea, to have given its interpretation.[62]

LE DIMANCHE.
PARIS.

IT was Sunday; and when La Fleur came in, in the morning, with my coffee and role and butter, he had got himself so gallantly array'd, I scarce knew him.

I had covenanted at Montriul to give him a new hat with a silver button and loop, and four Louis d'ors *pour s'adoniser*,[63] when we got to Paris; and the poor fellow, to do him justice, had done wonders with it.

He had bought a bright, clean, good scarlet coat and a pair of breeches of the same—They were not a crown worse, he said, for the wearing—I wish'd him hang'd for telling me—they look'd so fresh, that tho' I knew the thing could not be done, yet I would rather have imposed upon my fancy with thinking I had bought them new for the fellow, than that they had come out of the *Rue de friperie*.[64]

This is a nicety which makes not the heart sore at Paris.

He had purchased moreover a handsome blue sattin waistcoat, fancifully enough embroidered—this was indeed something the worse for the services, it had done, but 'twas clean scour'd—the gold had been touch'd up, and upon the whole was rather showy than otherwise—and as the blue was not violent, it suited with the coat and breeches very well: he had squeez'd out of the money, moreover, a new bag and a solitaire;[65] and had insisted with the *fripier*, upon a gold pair of garters to his breeches knees—He had purchased muslin ruffles, *bien brodées*,[66] with four livres of his own money—and a pair of white silk stockings for five more—and, to top all, nature had given him a handsome figure, without costing him a sous.

He enter'd the room thus set off, with his hair dress'd in the first

stile, and with a handsome *bouquet* in his breast—in a word, there was
that look of festivity in every thing about him, which at once put me
in mind it was Sunday—and by combining both together, it instantly
struck me, that the favour he wish'd to ask of me the night before, was
to spend the day, as every body in Paris spent it, besides. I had scarce
made the conjecture, when La Fleur, with infinite humility, but with a
look of trust, as if I should not refuse him, begg'd I would grant him
the day, *pour faire le galant vis à vis de sa maitresse.*[67]

Now it was the very thing I intended to do myself *vis à vis* Madame
de R****—I had retain'd the *remise* on purpose for it, and it would not
have mortified my vanity to have had a servant so well dress'd as La
Fleur was to have got up behind it: I never could have worse spared him.

But we must *feel*, not argue in these embarrassments—the sons and
daughters of service part with liberty, but not with Nature in their
contracts; they are flesh and blood, and have their little vanities and
wishes in the midst of the house of bondage,[68] as well as their task-
masters—no doubt, they have set their self-denials at a price—and
their expectations are so unreasonable, that I would often disappoint
them, but that their condition puts it so much in my power to do it.

Behold!—Behold, I am thy servant[69]—disarms me at once of the powers
of a master—

—Thou shalt go, La Fleur! said I.

—And what mistress, La Fleur, said I, canst thou have pick'd up in so
little a time at Paris? La Fleur laid his hand upon his breast, and said 'twas
a *petite demoiselle* at Monsieur Le Compte de B****'s.—La Fleur had a
heart made for society; and, to speak the truth of him let as few occasions
slip him as his master—so that some how or other; but how—heaven
knows—he had connected himself with the *demoiselle* upon the landing
of the stair-case, during the time I was taken up with my Passport; and
as there was time enough for me to win the Count to my interest, La
Fleur had contrived to make it do to win the maid to his—the family, it
seems, was to be at Paris that day, and he had made a party with her, and
two or three more of the Count's houshold, upon the *boulevards.*

Happy people! that once a week at least are sure to lay down all
your cares together; and dance and sing and sport away the weights of
grievance, which bow down the spirit of other nations to the earth.

THE FRAGMENT.
PARIS.

L A Fleur had left me something to amuse myself with for the day more than I had bargain'd for, or could have enter'd either into his head or mine.

He had brought the little print of butter upon a currant leaf; and as the morning was warm, and he had a good step to bring it, he had begg'd a sheet of waste paper to put betwixt the currant leaf and his hand—As that was plate sufficient, I bad him lay it upon the table as it was, and as I resolved to stay within all day I ordered him to call upon the *traiteur*[70] to bespeak my dinner, and leave me to breakfast by myself.

When I had finish'd the butter, I threw the currant leaf out of the window, and was going to do the same by the waste paper—but stopping to read a line first, and that drawing me on to a second and third—I thought it better worth; so I shut the window, and drawing a chair up to it, I sat down to read it.

It was in the old French of Rabelais's time,[71] and for ought I know might have been wrote by him—it was moreover in a Gothic letter, and that so faded and gone off by damps and length of time, it cost me infinite trouble to make any thing of it—I threw it down; and then wrote a letter to Eugenius—then I took it up again, and embroiled my patience with it afresh—and then to cure that, I wrote a letter to Eliza.—Still it kept hold of me; and the difficulty of understanding it increased but the desire.

I got my dinner; and after I had enlightened my mind with a bottle of Burgundy, I at it again—and after two or three hours poring upon it, with almost as deep attention as ever Gruter or Jacob Spon did upon a nonsensical inscription,[72] I thought I made sense of it; but to make sure of it, the best way, I imagined, was to turn it into English, and see how it would look then—so I went on leisurely, as a trifling man does, sometimes writing a sentence—then taking a turn or two—and then

97

looking how the world went, out of the window; so that it was nine o'clock
at night before I had done it—I then begun and read it as follows.

THE FRAGMENT.
PARIS.

——Now as the notary's wife disputed the point with the notary
with too much heat—I wish, said the notary, throwing down the
parchment, that there was another notary here only to set down and
attest all this——

—And what would you do then, Monsieur? said she, rising hastily
up—the notary's wife was a little fume of a woman, and the notary
thought it well to avoid a hurricane by a mild reply—I would go,
answer'd he, to bed.—— You may go to the devil, answer'd the notary's
wife.

Now there happening to be but one bed in the house, the other two
rooms being unfurnish'd, as is the custom at Paris, and the notary not
caring to lie in the same bed with a woman who had but that moment
sent him pell-mell to the devil, went forth with his hat and cane and
short cloak, the night being very windy, and walk'd out ill at ease
towards the *pont neuf.*

Of all the bridges which ever were built, the whole world who have
pass'd over the *pont neuf,* must own, that it is the noblest—the finest—
the grandest—the lightest—the longest—the broadest that ever con-
join'd land and land together upon the face of the terraqueous
globe——

By this, it seems, as if the author of the fragment had not been a Frenchman.

The worst fault which divines and the doctors of the Sorbonne can
allege against it, is, that if there is but a cap-full of wind in or about
Paris, 'tis more blasphemously *sacre Dieu*'d there than in any other

aperture of the whole city—and with reason, good and cogent Messieurs; for it comes against you without crying *garde d'eau*,[73] and with such unpremeditable puffs, that of the few who cross it with their hats on, not one in fifty but hazards two livres and a half, which is its full worth.

The poor notary, just as he was passing by the sentry, instinctively clapp'd his cane to the side of it, but in raising it up, the point of his cane catching hold of the loop of the sentinel's hat hoisted it over the spikes of the ballustrade clear into the Seine—

— '*Tis an ill wind*, said a boatsman, who catch'd it, *which blows no body any good.*

The sentry being a gascon incontinently twirl'd up his whiskers, and levell'd his harquebuss.[74]

Harquebusses in those days went off with matches; and an old woman's paper lanthorn at the end of the bridge happening to be blown out, she had borrow'd the sentry's match to light it—it gave a moment's time for the gascon's blood to run cool, and turn the accident better to his advantage— '*Tis an ill wind*, said he, catching off the notary's castor,[75] and legitimating the capture with the boatman's adage.

The poor notary cross'd the bridge, and passing along the rue de Dauphine into the fauxbourgs[76] of St. Germain, lamented himself as he walk'd along in this manner:

Luckless man! that I am, said the notary, to be the sport of hurricanes all my days—— to be born to have the storm of ill language levell'd against me and my profession wherever I go—to be forced into marriage by the thunder of the church to a tempest of a woman—to be driven forth out of my house by domestic winds, and despoil'd of my castor by pontific[77] ones—to be here, bare-headed, in a windy night at the mercy of the ebbs and flows of accidents—where am I to lay my head?—miserable man! what wind in the two-and-thirty points of the whole compass can blow unto thee, as it does to the rest of thy fellow creatures, good!

As the notary was passing on by a dark passage, complaining in this sort, a voice call'd out to a girl, to bid her run for the next notary— now the notary being the next, and availing himself of his situation, walk'd up the passage to the door, and passing through an old sort of a saloon; was usher'd into a large chamber dismantled of every thing but a long military pike—a breast plate—a rusty old sword, and bandoleer,[78] hung up equi-distant in four different places against the wall.

An old personage, who had heretofore been a gentleman, and unless decay of fortune taints the blood along with it was a gentleman at that time, lay supporting his head upon his hand in his bed; a little table with a taper burning was set close beside it, and close by the table was placed a chair—the notary sat him down in it; and pulling out his ink-horn and a sheet or two of paper which he had in his pocket, he placed them before him, and dipping his pen in his ink, and leaning his breast over the table, he disposed every thing to make the gentleman's last will and testament.

Alas! Monsieur le Notaire, said the gentleman, raising himself up a little, I have nothing to bequeath which will pay the expence of bequeathing, except the history of myself, which, I could not die in peace unless I left it as a legacy to the world; the profits arising out of it, I bequeath to you for the pains of taking it from me—it is a story so uncommon, it must be read by all mankind—it will make the fortunes of your house—the notary dipp'd his pen into his ink-horn— Almighty director of every event in my life! said the old gentleman, looking up earnestly and raising his hands towards heaven—thou whose hand has led me on through such a labyrinth of strange passages down into this scene of desolation, assist the decaying memory of an old, infirm, and broken-hearted man—direct my tongue, by the spirit of thy eternal truth, that this stranger may set down naught but what is written in that BOOK, from whose records, said he, clasping his hands together, I am to be condemn'd or acquitted![79] —— the notary held up the point of his pen betwixt the taper and his eye—

—It is a story, Monsieur le Notaire, said the gentleman, which will rouse up every affection in nature—it will kill the humane, and touch the heart of cruelty herself with pity—

—The notary was inflamed with a desire to begin, and put his pen a third time into his ink-horn—and the old gentleman turning a little more towards the notary, began to dictate his story in these words—

—And where is the rest of it, La Fleur? said I, as he just then enter'd the room.

THE FRAGMENT
AND THE *BOUQUET.
PARIS.

WHEN La Fleur came up close to the table, and was made to comprehend what I wanted, he told me there were only two other sheets of it which he had wrapt round the stalks of a *bouquet* to keep it together, which he had presented to the *demoiselle* upon the *boulevards*—Then, prithee, La Fleur, said I, step back to her to the Count de B****'s hotel, and *see if you canst get*—There is no doubt of it, said La Fleur—and away he flew.

In a very little time the poor fellow came back quite out of breath, with deeper marks of disappointment in his looks than could arise from the simple irreparability of the fragment—*Juste ciel!* in less than two minutes that the poor fellow had taken his last tender farewel of her—his faithless mistress had given his *gage d'amour*[80] to one of the Count's footmen—the footman to a young sempstress—and the sempstress to a fiddler, with my fragment at the end of it—Our misfortunes were involved together—I gave a sigh—and La Fleur echo'd it back again to my ear—

—How perfidious! cried La Fleur—How unlucky! said I.—

—I should not have been mortified, Monsieur, quoth La Fleur, if she had lost it—Nor I, La Fleur, said I, had I found it.

Whether I did or no, will be seen hereafter.

* Nosegay.

THE ACT OF CHARITY.
PARIS.

THE man who either disdains or fears to walk up a dark entry may be an excellent good man, and fit for a hundred things; but he will not do to make a good sentimental traveller. I count little of the many things I see pass at broad noon day, in large and open streets.—Nature is shy, and hates to act before spectators; but in such an unobserved corner, you sometimes see a single short scene of her's worth all the sentiments of a dozen French plays compounded together—and yet they are *absolutely* fine;—and whenever I have a more brilliant affair upon my hands than common, as they suit a preacher just as well as a hero, I generally make my sermon out of 'em—and for the text—"Capadosia, Pontus and Asia, Phrygia and Pamphilia"—is as good as any one in the Bible.[81]

There is a long dark passage issuing out from the opera comique into a narrow street; 'tis trod by a few who humbly wait for a *fiacre**, or wish to get off quietly o'foot when the opera is done. At the end of it, towards the theatre, 'tis lighted by a small candle, the light of which is almost lost before you get half-way down, but near the door—'tis more for ornament than use: you see it as a fix'd star of the least magnitude; it burns—but does little good to the world, that we know of.

In returning along this passage, I discern'd, as I approach'd within five or six paces of the door, two ladies standing arm in arm, with their backs against the wall, waiting, as I imagined, for a *fiacre*—as they were next the door, I thought they had a prior right; so edged myself up within a yard or little more of them, and quietly took my stand—I was in black, and scarce seen.

The lady next me was a tall lean figure of a woman of about thirty-six; the other of the same size and make, of about forty; there was no mark of wife or widow in any one part of either of them—they

---

* Hackney-coach.

seem'd to be two upright vestal sisters, unsapp'd by caresses, unbroke in upon by tender salutations: I could have wish'd to have made them happy—their happiness was destin'd, that night, to come from another quarter.

A low voice, with a good turn of expression, and sweet cadence at the end of it, begg'd for a twelve-sous piece betwixt them, for the love of heaven. I thought it singular, that a beggar should fix the quota of an alms—and that the sum should be twelve times as much as what is usually given in the dark. They both seemed astonish'd at it as much as myself.—Twelve sous! said one—a twelve-sous piece! said the other—and made no reply.

The poor man said, He knew not how to ask less of ladies of their rank; and bow'd down his head to the ground.

Poo! said they—we have no money.

The beggar remained silent for a moment or two, and renew'd his supplication.

Do not, my fair young ladies, said he, stop your good ears against me—Upon my word, honest man! said the younger, we have no change—Then God bless you, said the poor man, and multiply those joys which you can give to others without change!—I observed the elder sister put her hand into her pocket—I'll see, said she, if I have a sous.—A sous! give twelve, said the supplicant; Nature has been bountiful to you, be bountiful to a poor man.

I would, friend, with all my heart, said the younger, if I had it.

My fair charitable! said he, addressing himself to the elder—What is it but your goodness and humanity which makes your bright eyes so sweet, that they outshine the morning even in this dark passage? and what was it which made the Marquis de Santerre and his brother say so much of you both as they just pass'd by?

The two ladies seemed much affected; and impulsively at the same time they both put their hands into their pocket, and each took out a twelve-sous piece.

The contest betwixt them and the poor supplicant was no more—it was continued betwixt themselves, which of the two should give the twelve-sous piece in charity—and to end the dispute, they both gave it together, and the man went away.

The Riddle Explained.
PARIS.

I Stepp'd hastily after him: it was the very man whose success in asking charity of the women before the door of the hotel had so puzzled me—and I found at once his secret, or at least the basis of it—'twas flattery.

Delicious essence! how refreshing art thou to nature! how strongly are all its powers and all its weaknesses on thy side! how sweetly dost thou mix with the blood, and help it through the most difficult and tortuous passages to the heart!

The poor man, as he was not straighten'd for time, had given it here in a larger dose: 'tis certain he had a way of bringing it into less form, for the many sudden cases he had to do with in the streets; but how he contrived to correct, sweeten, concentre,[82] and qualify it—I vex not my spirit with the inquiry—it is enough, the beggar gain'd two twelve-sous pieces—and they can best tell the rest, who have gain'd much greater matters by it.

PARIS.

W E get forwards in the world not so much by doing services, as receiving them: you take a withering twig, and put it in the ground; and then you water it, because you have planted it.

Mons. Le Compte de B****, merely because he had done me one kindness in the affair of my passport, would go on and do me another, the few days he was at Paris, in making me known to a few people of rank; and they were to present me to others, and so on.

I had got master of my *secret*, just in time to turn these honours to some little account; otherwise, as is commonly the case, I should have din'd or supp'd a single time or two round, and then by *translating* French looks and attitudes into plain English, I should presently have seen, that I had got hold of the *couvert** of some more entertaining guest; and in course, should have resigned all my places one after another, merely upon the principle that I could not keep them.—As it was, things did not go much amiss.

I had the honour of being introduced to the old Marquis de B****: in days of yore he had signaliz'd himself by some small feats of chivalry in the *Cour d'amour*,[83] and had dress'd himself out to the idea of tilts and tournaments ever since—the Marquis de B**** wish'd to have it thought the affair was somewhere else than in his brain. "He could like to take a trip to England," and ask'd much of the English ladies. Stay where you are, I beseech you, Mons. le Marquise, said I—Les Messrs. Angloise can scarce get a kind look from them as it is.—The Marquis invited me to supper.

Mons. P**** the farmer-general was just as inquisitive about our taxes.—They were very considerable, he heard—If we knew but how to collect them, said I, making him a low bow.

I could never have been invited to Mons. P****'s concerts upon any other terms.[84]

I had been misrepresented to Madame de Q*** as an *esprit*[85]— Madam de Q*** was an *esprit* herself; she burnt with impatience to see me, and hear me talk. I had not taken my seat, before I saw she did not care a sous whether I had any wit or no—I was let in, to be convinced she had.—I call heaven to witness I never once open'd the door of my lips.

Madame de Q*** vow'd to every creature she met, "She had never had a more improving conversation with a man in her life."

There are three epochas in the empire of a French-woman—She is coquette—then deist—then *devôte*:[86] the empire during these is never lost—she only changes her subjects: when thirty-five years and more have unpeopled her dominions of the slaves of love, she re-peoples it with slaves of infidelity—and then with the slaves of the Church.

Madame de V*** was vibrating betwixt the first of these epochas:

---

* Plate, napkin, knife, fork, and spoon.

the colour of the rose was shading fast away—she ought to have been a deist five years before the time I had the honour to pay my first visit.

She placed me upon the same sopha with her, for the sake of disputing the point of religion more closely.—In short, Madame de V*** told me she believed nothing.

I told Madame de V*** it might be her principle; but I was sure it could not be her interest to level the outworks, without which I could not conceive how such a citadel as hers could be defended—that there was not a more dangerous thing in the world, than for a beauty to be a deist—that it was a debt I owed my creed, not to conceal it from her—that I had not been five minutes sat upon the sopha besides her, but I had begun to form designs—and what is it, but the sentiments of religion, and the persuasion they had existed in her breast, which could have check'd them as they rose up.

We are not adamant, said I, taking hold of her hand—and there is need of all restraints, till age in her own time steals in and lays them on us—but, my dear lady, said I, kissing her hand—'tis too—too soon—

I declare I had the credit all over Paris of unperverting Madame de V***.—She affirmed to Mons. D*** and the Abbe M***, that in one half hour I had said more for revealed religion, than all their Encyclopedia had said against it[87]—I was listed directly into Madame de V***'s *Coterie*—and she put off the epocha of deism for two years.

I remember it was in this *Coterie*, in the middle of a discourse, in which I was shewing the necessity of a *first cause*, that the young Count de Faineant[88] took me by the hand to the furthest corner of the room, to tell me my *solitaire* was pinn'd too strait about my neck—It should be *plus badinant*,[89] said the Count, looking down upon his own—but a word, Mons. Yorick, to *the wise*—

—And from the wise, Mons. Le Compte, replied I, making him a bow—*is enough.*

The Count de Faineant embraced me with more ardour than ever I was embraced by mortal man.

For three weeks together, I was of every man's opinion I met.— *Pardi! ce Mons. Yorick a autant d'esprit que nous autres.*——*Il raisonne bien,* said another.—*C'est un bon enfant,*[90] said a third.—And at this price I could have eaten and drank and been merry all the days of my life at

Paris; but 'twas a dishonest *reckoning*—I grew ashamed of it—it was the gain of a slave—every sentiment of honour revolted against it—the higher I got, the more was I forced upon my *beggarly system*—the better the *Coterie*—the more children of Art—I languish'd for those of Nature: and one night, after a most vile prostitution of myself to half a dozen different people, I grew sick—went to bed—order'd La Fleur to get me horses in the morning to set out for Italy.

MARIA.
MOULINES.

I NEVER felt what the distress of plenty was in any one shape till now—to travel it through the Bourbonnois, the sweetest part of France—in the hey-day of the vintage, when Nature is pouring her abundance into every one's lap, and every eye is lifted up—a journey through each step of which music beats time to *Labour*, and all her children are rejoicing as they carry in their clusters—to pass through this with my affections flying out, and kindling at every group before me—and every one of 'em was pregnant with adventures.

Just heaven!—it would fill up twenty volumes—and alas! I have but a few small pages left of this to croud it into—and half of these must be taken up with the poor Maria my friend, Mr. Shandy, met with near Moulines.[91]

The story he had told of that disorder'd maid affect'd me not a little in the reading; but when I got within the neighbourhood where she lived, it returned so strong into my mind, that I could not resist an impulse which prompted me to go half a league out of the road to the village where her parents dwelt to enquire after her.

'Tis going, I own, like the Knight of the Woeful Countenance,[92] in quest of melancholy adventures—but I know not how it is, but I am never so perfectly conscious of the existence of a soul within me, as when I am entangled in them.

The old mother came to the door, her looks told me the story before she open'd her mouth—She had lost her husband; he had died, she said, of anguish, for the loss of Maria's senses about a month before.— She had feared at first, she added, that it would have plunder'd her poor girl of what little understanding was left—but, on the contrary, it had brought her more to herself—still she could not rest—her poor daughter, she said, crying, was wandering somewhere about the road—

—Why does my pulse beat languid as I write this? and what made La Fleur, whose heart seem'd only to be tuned to joy, to pass the back of his hand twice across his eyes, as the woman stood and told it? I beckon'd to the postilion to turn back into the road.

When we had got within half a league of Moulines, at a little opening in the road leading to a thicket, I discovered poor Maria sitting under a poplar—she was sitting with her elbow in her lap, and her head leaning on one side within her hand—a small brook ran at the foot of the tree.

I bid the postilion go on with the chaise to Moulines—and La Fleur to bespeak my supper—and that I would walk after him.

She was dress'd in white, and much as my friend described her, except that her hair hung loose, which before was twisted within a silk net.—She had, superadded likewise to her jacket, a pale green ribband which fell across her shoulder to the waist; at the end of which hung her pipe.—Her goat had been as faithless as her lover; and she had got a little dog in lieu of him, which she had kept tied by a string to her girdle; as I look'd at her dog, she drew him towards her with the string.—"Thou shalt not leave me, Sylvio," said she.[93] I look'd in Maria's eyes, and saw she was thinking more of her father than of her lover or her little goat; for as she utter'd them the tears trickled down her cheeks.

I sat down close by her; and Maria let me wipe them away as they fell with my handkerchief.—I then steep'd it in my own—and then in hers—and then in mine—and then I wip'd hers again—and as I did it, I felt such undescribable emotions within me, as I am sure could not be accounted for from any combinations of matter and motion.

I am positive I have a soul; nor can all the books with which materialists have pester'd the world ever convince me of the contrary.

their full understanding,

MARIA.

WHEN Maria had come a little to herself, I ask'd her if she remember'd a pale thin person of a man who had sat down betwixt her and her goat about two years before? She said, she was unsettled much at that time, but remember'd it upon two accounts— that ill as she was she saw the person pitied her; and next, that her goat had stolen his handkerchief, and she had beat him for the theft—she had wash'd it, she said, in the brook, and kept it ever since in her pocket to restore it to him in case she should ever see him again, which, she added, he had half promised her. As she told me this, she took the handkerchief out of her pocket to let me see it; she had folded it up neatly in a couple of vine leaves, tied round with a tendril—on opening it, I saw an S mark'd in one of the corners.

She had since that, she told me, stray'd as far as Rome, and walk'd round St. Peter's once—and return'd back—that she found her way alone across the Apennines—had travell'd over all Lombardy without money—and through the flinty roads of Savoy without shoes—how she had borne it, and how she had got supported, she could not tell— but *God tempers the wind*, said Maria, to the shorn lamb.[94]

Shorn indeed! and to the quick, said I; and wast thou in my own land, where I have a cottage, I would take thee to it and shelter thee: thou shouldst eat of my own bread, and drink of my own cup[95]—I would be kind to thy Sylvio—in all thy weaknesses and wanderings I would seek after thee and bring thee back—when the sun went down I would say my prayers, and when I had done thou shouldst play thy evening song upon thy pipe, nor would the incense of my sacrifice be worse accepted[96] for entering heaven along with that of a broken heart.

Nature melted within me, as I utter'd this; and Maria observing, as I took out my handkerchief, that it was steep'd too much already to be of use, would needs go wash it in the stream.—And where will you dry it, Maria? said I—I'll dry it in my bosom, said she—'twill do me good.

And is your heart still so warm, Maria? said I.

I touch'd upon the string on which hung all her sorrows—she look'd with wistful disorder for some time in my face; and then, without saying any thing, took her pipe, and play'd her service to the Virgin—The string I had touch'd ceased to vibrate—in a moment or two Maria returned to herself—let her pipe fall—and rose up.

And where art you going, Maria? said I.—She said to Moulines.—Let us go, said I, together.—Maria put her arm within mine, and lengthening the string, to let the dog follow—in that order we entered Moulines.

MARIA.
MOULINES.

THO' I hate salutations and greetings in the market-place,[97] yet when we got into the middle of this, I stopp'd to take my last look and last farewel of Maria.

Maria, tho' not tall, was nevertheless of the first order of fine forms—affliction had touch'd her looks with something that was scarce earthly—still she was feminine—and so much was there about her of all that the heart wishes, or the eye looks for in woman, that could the traces be ever worn out of her brain, and those of Eliza's out of mine, she should *not only eat of my bread and drink of my own cup*, but Maria should lay in my bosom, and be unto me as a daughter.[98]

Adieu, poor luckless maiden!—imbibe the oil and wine which the compassion of a stranger, as he journieth on his way, now pours into thy wounds—the being who has twice bruised thee can only bind them up for ever.[99]

THE BOURBONNOIS.

THERE was nothing from which I had painted out for myself so joyous a riot of the affections, as in this journey in the vintage, through this part of France; but pressing through this gate of sorrow to it, my sufferings had totally unfitted me: in every scene of festivity I saw Maria in the back-ground of the piece, sitting pensive under her poplar; and I had got almost to Lyons before I was able to cast a shade across her—

—Dear sensibility! source inexhausted of all that's precious in our joys, or costly in our sorrows! thou chainest thy martyr down upon his bed of straw—and 'tis thou who lifts him up to HEAVEN—eternal fountain of our feelings!—'tis here I trace thee—and this is thy divinity which stirs within me —— not, that in some sad and sickening moments, "*my soul shrinks back upon herself, and startles at destruction*"[100]— mere pomp of words!—but that I feel some generous joys and generous cares beyond myself—all comes from thee, great—great SENSORIUM of the world! which vibrates, if a hair of our heads but falls upon the ground,[101] in the remotest desert of thy creation.—Touch'd with thee, Eugenius draws my curtain[102] when I languish—hears my tale of symptoms, and blames the weather for the disorder of his nerves. Thou giv'st a portion of it sometimes to the roughest peasant who traverses the bleakest mountains—he finds the lacerated lamb of another's flock—This moment I beheld him leaning with his head against his crook, with piteous inclination looking down upon it—Oh! had I come one moment sooner!—it bleeds to death—his gentle heart bleeds with it—

Peace to thee, generous swain!—I see thou walkest off with anguish—but thy joys shall balance it—for happy is thy cottage—and happy is the sharer of it—and happy are the lambs which sport about you.

THE SUPPER.

A SHOE coming loose from the fore-foot of the thill-horse,[103] at the beginning of the ascent of mount Taurira, the postilion dismounted, twisted the shoe off, and put it in his pocket; as the ascent was of five or six miles, and that horse our main dependence, I made a point of having the shoe fasten'd on again, as well as we could; but the postilion had thrown away the nails, and the hammer in the chaise-box, being of no great use without them, I submitted to go on.

He had not mounted half a mile higher, when coming to a flinty piece of road, the poor devil lost a second shoe, and from off his other fore-foot; I then got out of the chaise in good earnest; and seeing a house about a quarter of a mile to the left-hand, with a great deal to do, I prevailed upon the postilion to turn up to it. The look of the house, and of every thing about it, as we drew nearer, soon reconciled me to the disaster.—It was a little farm-house surrounded with about twenty acres of vineyard, about as much corn—and close to the house, on one side, was a *potagerie*[104] of an acre and a half, full of every thing which could make plenty in a French peasant's house—and on the other side was a little wood which furnished wherewithal to dress it. It was about eight in the evening when I got to the house—so I left the postilion to manage his point as he could—and for mine, I walk'd directly into the house.

The family consisted of an old grey-headed man and his wife, with five or six sons and sons-in-law and their several wives, and a joyous genealogy out of 'em.

They were all sitting down together to their lentil-soup; a large wheaten loaf was in the middle of the table; and a flaggon of wine at each end of it promised joy thro' the stages of the repast—'twas a feast of love.

The old man rose up to meet me, and with a respectful cordiality would have me sit down at the table; my heart was sat down the moment I enter'd the room; so I sat down at once like a son of the family; and to invest myself in the character as speedily as I could, I instantly borrowed the old man's knife, and taking up the loaf cut myself a hearty luncheon; and as I did it I saw a testimony in every eye, not only of an honest welcome, but of a welcome mix'd with thanks that I had not seem'd to doubt it.

Was it this; or tell me, Nature, what else it was which made this morsel so sweet—and to what magick I owe it, that the draught I took of their flaggon was so delicious with it, that they remain upon my palate to this hour?

If the supper was to my taste—the grace which follow'd it was much more so.

Dancing = celebration of the physical

THE GRACE.

WHEN supper was over, the old man gave a knock upon the table with the haft of his knife—to bid them prepare for the dance: the moment the signal was given, the women and girls ran all together into a back apartment to tye up their hair—and the young men to the door to wash their faces, and change their sabots;[105] and in three minutes every soul was ready upon a little esplanade before the house to begin—The old man and his wife came out last, and, placing me betwixt them, sat down upon a sopha of turf by the door.

The old man had some fifty years ago been no mean performer upon the vielle[106]—and at the age he was then of, touch'd it well enough for the purpose. His wife sung now-and-then a little to the tune—then intermitted—and joined her old man again as their children and grand-children danced before them.

It was not till the middle of the second dance, when, from some pauses in the movement wherein they all seemed to look up, I fancied I could distinguish an elevation of spirit different from that which is the cause or the effect of simple jollity.—In a word, I thought I beheld *Religion* mixing in the dance—but as I had never seen her so engaged, I should have look'd upon it now, as one of the illusions of an imagination which is eternally misleading me, had not the old man, as soon as the dance ended, said, that this was their constant way; and that all his life long he had made it a rule, after supper was over, to call out his family to dance and rejoice; believing, he said, that a chearful and contented mind was the best sort of thanks to heaven that an illiterate peasant could pay—[107]

—— Or a learned prelate either, said I.

THE CASE OF DELICACY. [108]

WHEN you have gained the top of mount Taurira, you run presently down to Lyons—adieu then to all rapid movements! 'Tis a journey of caution; and it fares better with sentiments, not to be in a hurry with them; so I contracted with a Voiturin[109] to take his time with a couple of mules, and convey me in my own chaise safe to Turin through Savoy.

Poor, patient, quiet, honest people! fear not; your poverty, the treasury of your simple virtues, will not be envied you by the world, nor will your vallies be invaded by it.—Nature! in the midst of thy disorders, thou art still friendly to the scantiness thou hast created—with all thy great works about thee, little hast thou left to give, either to the scithe or to the sickle—but to that little, thou grantest safety and protection; and sweet are the dwellings which stand so shelter'd.

Let the way-worn traveller vent his complaints upon the sudden turns and dangers of your roads—your rocks—your precipices—the difficulties of getting up—the horrors of getting down—mountains impracticable—and cataracts, which roll down great stones from their summits, and block his road up.—The peasants had been all day at work in removing a fragment of this kind between St. Michael and Madane; and by the time my Voiturin got to the place, it wanted full two hours of compleating before a passage could any how be gain'd: there was nothing but to wait with patience—'twas a wet and tempestuous night; so that by the delay, and that together, the Voiturin found himself obliged to take up five miles short of his stage at a little decent kind of an inn by the road side.

I forthwith took possession of my bed-chamber—got a good fire—order'd supper; and was thanking heaven it was no worse—when a voiture arrived with a lady in it and her servant-maid.[110]

As there was no other bed-chamber in the house, the hostess, without much nicety, led them into mine, telling them, as she usher'd them in, that there was no body in it but an English gentleman—that there were two good beds in it, and a closet within the room which held another—the accent in which she spoke of this third bed did not say much for it—however, she said, there were three beds, and but three people—and she durst say, the gentleman would do any thing to accommodate matters.—I left not the lady a moment to make a conjecture about it—so instantly made a declaration I would do any thing in my power.

As this did not amount to an absolute surrender of my bed-chamber, I still felt myself so much the proprietor, as to have a right to do the honours of it—so I desired the lady to sit down—pressed her into the warmest seat—call'd for more wood—desired the hostess to enlarge the plan of the supper, and to favour us with the very best wine.

The lady had scarce warm'd herself five minutes at the fire, before she began to turn her head back, and give a look at the beds; and the oftener she cast her eyes that way, the more they return'd perplex'd—I felt for her—and for myself; for in a few minutes, what by her looks, and the case itself, I found myself as much embarrassed as it was possible the lady could be herself.

That the beds we were to lay in were in one and the same room, was enough simply by itself to have excited all this—but the position of them, for they stood parallel, and so very close to each other as only to allow space for a small wicker chair betwixt them, render'd the affair still more oppressive to us—they were fixed up moreover near the fire, and the projection of the chimney on one side, and a large beam which cross'd the room on the other, form'd a kind of recess for them that was no way favourable to the nicety of our sensations—if any thing could have added to it, it was, that the two beds were both of 'em so very small, as to cut us off from every idea of the lady and the maid lying together; which in either of them, could it have been feasible, my lying besides them, tho' a thing not to be wish'd, yet there was nothing in it so terrible which the imagination might not have pass'd over without torment.

As for the little room within, it offer'd little or no consolation to us; 'twas a damp cold closet, with a half dismantled window shutter, and with a window which had neither glass or oil paper in it to keep out the tempest of the night. I did not endeavour to stifle my cough when the lady gave a peep into it; so it reduced the case in course to this alternative—that the lady should sacrifice her health to her feelings, and take up with the closet herself, and abandon the bed next mine to her maid—or that the girl should take the closet, &c. &c.

The lady was a Piedmontese of about thirty, with a glow of health in her cheeks.—The maid was a Lyonoise of twenty, and as brisk and lively a French girl as ever moved.—There were difficulties every way—and the obstacle of the stone in the road, which brought us into the distress, great as it appeared whilst the peasants were removing it, was but a pebble to what lay in our ways now—I have only to add, that it did not lessen the weight which hung upon our spirits, that we were both too delicate to communicate what we felt to each other upon the occasion.

We sat down to supper; and had we not had more generous wine to it than a little inn in Savoy could have furnish'd, our tongues had been tied up, till necessity herself had set them at liberty—but the lady having a few bottles of Burgundy in her voiture sent down her Fille de Chambre for a couple of them; so that by the time supper was over, and we were left alone, we felt ourselves inspired with a strength of mind sufficient to talk, at least, without reserve upon our situation. We turn'd it every way, and debated and considered it in all kind of lights in the course of a two hours negociation; at the end of which the articles were settled finally betwixt us, and stipulated for in form and manner of a treaty of peace—and I believe with as much religion and good faith on both sides, as in any treaty which as yet had the honour of being handed down to posterity.

They were as follows:

First. As the right of the bed-chamber is in Monsieur—and he thinking the bed next to the fire to be the warmest, he insists upon the concession on the lady's side of taking up with it.

Granted, on the part of Madame; with a proviso, That as the curtains of that bed are of a flimsy transparent cotton, and appear likewise too scanty to draw close, that the Fille de Chambre, shall fasten up the opening, either by corking pins,[111] or needle and thread, in such manner as shall be deemed a sufficient barrier on the side of Monsieur.

2dly. It is required on the part of Madame, that Monsieur shall lay the whole night through in his robe de chambre.

Rejected: inasmuch Monsieur is not worth a robe de chambre; he having nothing in his portmanteau but six shirts and a black silk pair of breeches.

The mentioning the silk pair of breeches made an entire change of the article—for the breeches were accepted as an equivalent for the robe de chambre, and so it was stipulated and agreed upon that I should lay in my black silk breeches all night.

3dly. It was insisted upon, and stipulated for by the lady, that after Monsieur was got to bed, and the candle and fire extinguished, that Monsieur should not speak one single word the whole night.

Granted; provided Monsieur's saying his prayers might not be deem'd an infraction of the treaty.

There was but one point forgot in this treaty, and that was the manner in which the lady and myself should be obliged to undress and get to bed—there was but one way of doing it, and that I leave to the reader to devise; protesting as I do it, that if it is not the most delicate in nature, 'tis the fault of his own imagination—against which this is not my first complaint.[112]

Now when we were got to bed, whether it was the novelty of the situation, or what it was, I know not; but so it was, I could not shut my eyes; I tried this side and that, and turn'd and turn'd again, till a full hour after midnight; when Nature and patience both wearing out—O my God! said I——

——You have broke the treaty, Monsieur, said the lady, who had no more slept than myself.—I begg'd a thousand pardons—but insisted it was no more than an ejaculation—she maintain'd 'twas an entire infraction of the treaty—I maintain'd it was provided for in the clause of the third article.

The lady would by no means give up her point, tho' she weakened her barrier by it; for in the warmth of the dispute, I could hear two or three corking pins fall out of the curtain to the ground.

Upon my word and honour, Madame, said I—stretching my arm out of bed, by way of asseveration—

—(I was going to have added, that I would not have trespass'd against the remotest idea of decorum for the world)—

—But the Fille de Chambre hearing there were words between us, and fearing that hostilities would ensue in course, had crept silently out of her closet, and it being totally dark, had stolen so close to our beds, that she had got herself into the narrow passage which separated them, and had advanc'd so far up as to be in a line betwixt her mistress and me—

So that when I stretch'd out my hand, I caught hold of the Fille de Chambre's

END OF VOL. II.[113]

Notes

In preparing these notes, I have drawn significantly on the work of previous annotators, particularly Gardner D. Stout, Jr (see Further Reading) and Tom Keymer, editor of *A Sentimental Journey and Other Writings* (London: J. M. Dent, 1994). I have also made use of material in Shaun Regan's doctoral thesis 'Laurence Sterne, Wit, and Politeness: Comedy and Cultural Politics in Eighteenth-Century England' (University of Wales, Aberystwyth, 2000).

Translations of Sterne's French are not always literal, but rather aim to capture the general sense of the (often inaccurate) original. Repeated words or expressions are translated only at the first occurrence. Where I have judged the meaning to be obvious, no translation is provided. Where there is a cluster of French phrases, translations are grouped in a single note following the final phrase.

Scripture is quoted from the Authorized Version. Titles often referred to or quoted from have been abbreviated as follows:

Cash, *LY* Arthur H. Cash, *Laurence Sterne: The Later Years* (London: Methuen, 1986).

Letters *Letters of Laurence Sterne*, ed. Lewis Perry Curtis (Oxford: Clarendon Press, 1935).

Sermons The Florida Edition of *The Works of Laurence Sterne*, vol. IV, ed. Melvyn New (Gainesville: University Press of Florida, 1996). When sermon numbers are given, they are from this edition.

SJ *A Sentimental Journey*.

Travels Tobias Smollett, *Travels through France and Italy*, ed. Frank Felsenstein (Oxford: Oxford University Press, 1981).

TS Sterne, *The Life and Opinions of Tristram Shandy, Gentleman*, ed. Melvyn New and Joan New (London: Penguin Books, 1997).

Notes to Volume I

1. *Advertisement*: Sterne's pledge to write more volumes was printed on a loose sheet inserted into subscription copies of the first edition (a list of the 281 subscribers followed the title-page). The promise was almost certainly genuine – Sterne had planned *SJ* as 'a new work of four volumes' (*Letters*, p. 284).

2. *packet*: Packet-boat, a regular service conveying mail, goods and passengers.

3. *Droits d'aubaine*: Literally 'Rights over stranger' (from ancient French). Sterne's footnote echoes Smollett's objection to the law (*Travels*, letter ii). The profits were 'farmed' in the sense that they were collected by the (often rapacious) *fermiers généraux* (farmers-general) (see n. 84 to vol. II). Sterne gained bitter personal experience of the law when he organized the funeral and effects of George Oswald, a young tourist who died near Toulouse in 1763 (see Peter de Voogd, 'The Oswald Papers', *The Shandean*, 10 (1998), pp. 80–91).

4. *Eliza*: Reference to Mrs Elizabeth Draper (see Introduction, p. xv). Sterne refers in the *Journal* to 'a portrait (which by the by, I have immortalized in my Sentimental Journey)' (*Letters*, p. 357). Sterne informed friends and correspondents of his relationship, so the reference would have been recognized by many readers.

5. *When man is at peace . . . called me a machine*: The association of good humour and physical health is common in Sterne's writing – cf., for example, sermon 5: 'nothing more contributes to health than a benevolence of temper' (*Sermons*, p. 49). A *précieuse* is a woman affecting refined language and taste (as satirized in Molière's *Les Précieuses ridicules* (1659), which popularized the term). Yorick's '*physical precieuse*' presumably follows fashionable materialistic philosophy, such as is put forward in La Mettrie's *L'Homme machine* (1748), according to which matter is seen to possess the capacity for thought (as opposed to 'dualist' philosophy which sees man as a composition of mind and matter or soul and body).

6. *sed non, quo ad hanc*: Ambiguous phrase meaning perhaps 'but not, as far as this (is concerned)'. Sterne was an accomplished Latinist, so the obscurity here is curious.

7. *Guido*: Guido Reni (1575–1642), Bolognese baroque painter of religious and mythological subjects, much admired by eighteenth-century travellers and connoisseurs. Smollett respected his works, though found that 'his expression is often erroneous, and his attitudes are always affected' (*Travels*, letter xxxi).

8. *Bramin*: A member of the Hindu priesthood, proverbially associated with wisdom. Sterne and Eliza used 'Bramin' and 'Bramine' as pet names (suggestive of Sterne's clerical status and Eliza's Indian associations).

9. *the order of mercy, instead of the order of St. Francis*: Contrasting the mendicant Franciscan order with the Order of Our Lady of Mercy, founded in 1218 to raise ransoms for Christians captured by the Moors during the crusades.

10. *we distinguish . . . for the love of God*: Denigration of Catholics and Catholicism is frequent in Sterne's sermons and in *TS* (especially the early volumes). Of particular relevance here is the definition of 'popery' in sermon 19: 'a pecuniary system, well contrived to operate upon men's passions and weakness, whilst their pockets are o'picking' (*Sermons*, p. 184).

11. *a hectic of a moment*: A momentary flush.

12. *Monsieur Dessein*: The Calais hotelkeeper Pierre Quillacq (1726–93), commonly called 'Dessin' and well known to English travellers. Sterne stayed at hotels run by him in 1762 and 1765. A keen entrepreneur, Dessein profited from exchanging currency and renting chaises, and he thrived on the added fame *SJ* brought him (see Cash, *LY*, p. 229).

13. *many a peripatetic philosopher*: Yorick drolly connects his own position as 'travelling observer' with the Aristotelian or peripatetic philosophical school (so called because of Aristotle's practice of teaching while walking).

14. *the efficient as well as the final causes*: I.e. the causes which produce effects and the underlying purposes.

15. *benefit of the clergy*: Literally, clerical immunity from ordinary jurisdiction, but here a reference to the use of clerics as governors of young aristocrats on the Grand Tour.

16. *besoin de Voyager*: 'Need to travel'.

17. *Mynheer*: Dutch equivalent of 'sir'; a Dutchman.

18. *discovering his nakedness*: An allusion to Noah (like Yorick's Dutchman, an innovative wine-grower) who is exposed after becoming drunk (Genesis 9:20–23).

19. *as Sancho Pança said . . . dry-shod at home*: Referring to Cervantes, *Don Quixote* (1605–15), Part II.v (where Sancho is in fact speaking with his wife).

20. *Where then, my dear countrymen, are you going*: Sterne based much of the preceding paragraph on Bishop Joseph Hall's *Quo Vadis? A Just Censure of Travel* (1617) – he translates and evokes the Latin of the title with this concluding question.

21. *Vis a Vis*: Carriage in which (usually) two passengers sit face to face.

22. *effectually*: In fact (from *en effet*).

23. *it had been twice taken to pieces on Mount Sennis*: To cross the Alps at Mount Cenis, on the French–Italian border, carriages were sometimes dismantled and carried on mules.

24. *Mon Dieu*: 'My God!'

25. *C'est bien vrai*: 'It's very true'.

26. *d'un homme d'esprit*: 'of a man of spirit'.

27. *Remise*: Coach-house (Sterne later uses 'remise' in its other sense of 'hired carriage').

28. *conventionist*: Someone entering into a contract.

29. *Hyde-park corner to fight a duel*: London's Hyde Park was a favoured venue for duelling, a practice still common in Sterne's time.

30. *en face*: 'Face on'.

31. *look'd like a Jew—then a Turk*: Jews and Turks were widely mistrusted in England as acquisitive and deceitful. Yorick seems to invoke such stereotypes to confirm his suspicions of Dessein.

32. *louis d'ors*: The louis d'or was a gold coin minted from 1640 until 1795, and was valued in the mid-eighteenth century at 24 livres (an idea of its value can be gauged from Yorick's wine 'at least of two livres a bottle' (p. 6).

33. *thy hand . . . against thee*: Cf. Genesis 16:12, where God's angel proclaims that Ishmael's 'hand *will be* against every man, and every man's hand against him'.

34. *diabled*: 'Cursed' (Sterne creates the verb from the exclamation '*Diable!*' meaning 'Devil!').

35. *the truth . . . whole truth*: Yorick seems to paraphrase the oath sworn by a witness in court as he confesses to his incomplete relation of the facts.

36. *for the drawing . . . into the Tiber for it*: Cf. Tristram's invitation to his reader to 'please but your own fancy' in picturing the Widow Wadman (*TS*, VI.xxxviii, pp. 388–90). The Tiber was known as an abundant source of archaeological remains, including statues of gods and goddesses.

37. *bon ton*: 'Good style'.

38. *Esdras . . . courtesy*: Esdras is a reputed author of the Apocrypha; Yorick paraphrases the words of a visiting angel comforting the prophet (2 Esdras 10:31). The benevolence of 'a certain poor widow' who 'threw in two mites, which make a farthing' is related in Mark 12:42 (see also Luke 21:2).

39. *neither oil nor wine to the wound*: Contrasting with Luke 10:34, in which the good Samaritan helps the thieves' victim by binding 'up his wounds, pouring in oil and wine'.

40. *tartufish*: Like the religious hypocrite of Molière's comedy *Tartuffe* (1664–9).

41. *Vous n'etez pas de Londre*: 'You are not from London?';
Apparamment vous etez Flammande: 'Apparently you are Flemish then?';
Peutetre, de Lisle: 'From Lisle perhaps?'.

42. *bombardment . . . by the French*: Brussels was besieged by the French in the War of the Austrian Succession (1740–48) and was won from the (English, Dutch and Austrian) Imperialist allies in 1746;
pour cela: 'For that purpose'.

43. *Et Madame a son Mari*: Either 'And Madame is with her husband?' or 'Is Madame married?'

44. *to chaffer*: To haggle/bargain.

45. *C'est bien comique*: 'It's very funny'.

46. *fort*: 'Strength'.

47. *pours and contres*: 'Pros and cons'.

48. *eyes to see . . . hands on*: Perhaps echoing Deuteronomy 29:4: 'the Lord hath not given you an heart to perceive, and eyes to see, and ears to hear, unto this day'; and Ecclesiastes 9:11: 'time and chance happeneth to them all' (Sterne addressed the latter text in sermon 8, 'Time and Chance', *Sermons*, pp. 74–80). Like Yorick, Tristram Shandy finds adventure in happenstantial details: 'by seizing every handle, of what size or shape soever, which chance held out to me in this journey—I turned my *plain* into a *city*' (*TS*, VII.xliii, p. 444).

49. *Dan to Beersheba*: I.e. a long way. Paraphrased from the biblical commonplace 'from Dan even to Beer-sheba', referring to the north and south boundaries of Canaan.

50. *Smelfungus*: Satirical portrait of Tobias Smollett (1721–71). See Introduction, pp. xviii–xx.

51. *the Pantheon . . . provocation in nature*: Smollett 'was much disappointed at sight of the Pantheon, which . . . looks like a huge cockpit, open at top' (*Travels*, letter xxxi). Of the Venus de Medicis he complained 'there is no beauty in the features . . . the attitude is aukward and out of character', but he enthused at length over 'the back parts' which 'are executed so happily, as to excite the admiration of the most indifferent spectator' (*Travels*, letter xxviii).

52. *wherein he spoke . . . the Anthropophagi*: Paraphrased from *Othello*, I.iii.134–44.

53. *flea'd alive . . . had come at*: Alluding to Smollett's disapproval of Rome's ecclesiastical paintings – 'the shocking subjects of the martyrology . . . Bartholomew flaed alive, and a hundred other pictures equally frightful' (*Travels*, letter xxxi), and probably punning so as to mock Smollett's numerous complaints about dirty, flea-ridden inns (or 'stages').

54. *Mundungus . . . out of his road*: Perhaps satirizing a specific traveller, although none has been definitely identified. Keymer suggests the character may represent a general type of *nouveau riche* traveller. Sterne may again have had negative comparisons with the Good Samaritan in mind (see n. 39 above), as in sermon 3, which contrasts the philanthropic Samaritan with the 'sordid wretch, whose straight heart is open to no man's affliction . . . he goes . . . in the same selfish track . . . turning neither to the right hand nor to the left . . . lest peradventure he should see aught which might turn him one moment out of that straight line where interest is carrying him——or if, by chance, he stumbles upon a hapless object of distress . . .' (*Sermons*, p. 24).

55. qu'un my Lord Anglois . . . Janatone: 'That an English Lord presented an *ecu* [a coin worth 6 livres] to the chambermaid – Too bad for Mademoiselle Janatone'. Cf. Tristram Shandy's rapid passage through Montreuil, where only Janatone, the inn-keeper's daughter, engages his attention (*TS*, VII.ix, pp. 404–5).

56. tant mieux: 'That's good/so much the better';

toujours: 'Always';

Pardonnez moi: 'Pardon me/forgive me'.

57. Mr. H . . . for both: The philosopher and historian David Hume (1711–76) and the poet and tragedian John Home, pronounced 'Hume' (1722–1808). Sterne met Hume in Paris in 1764 and commended his 'placid and gentle nature' (*Letters*, p. 218).

58. a ses terres: 'To his land';

comme il plaisoit a Dieu: 'as it pleases God'.

59. compagnon du voiage: 'Travelling companion';

equivoque: 'Play on words';

O qu'oui: 'O, but yes!'.

60. spatterdashes: Long gaiters for protecting the legs against the wet.

61. for whether 'twas hunger . . . journeyings: Cf. St Paul's account of his torments: 'stripes above measure . . . *In* journeyings often . . . in watchings often, in hunger and thirst . . . in cold and nakedness' (2 Corinthians 11:23–7).

62. C'est un garçon de bonne fortune: 'It's a boy of good fortune' (implying La Fleur's seductive powers as in the more usual *'homme à bonnes fortunes'* meaning 'ladykiller/ladies man').

63. eloge: 'Eulogy'.

64. A Fragment . . . reclaim it: Democritus (*c.* 460–370 BC), an inhabitant of Abdera, was known as 'the laughing philosopher' for his ironic amusement at mankind's foibles. The anecdote in the fragment is adapted from Robert Burton, *The Anatomy of Melancholy* (1621; 6th edn 1651), Part 3, Sect. 2, Memb. 2, Subsect. 4, which was published under the name 'Democritus Jr'.

65. pasquinades: Lampoons or satires displayed in public.

66. Andromeda of Euripedes: Lost tragedy, which, appropriately for this context, survives only in fragments.

67. orchestra: I.e. the audience in front of the stage (although in a Greek theatre the orchestra typically contained the chorus of singers and dancers).

68. helebore: Ancient name for various plants believed to cure madness.

69. parterre: Theatre stalls/the audience in those seats;

Place aux dames: 'Give way to the ladies'.

70. Prenez en—prenez: 'Take some – take'.

71. Vive le Roi: 'Long live the King!';

pour l'amour de Dieu: 'For the love of God';

Mon cher . . . Monsieur: 'My dear and very charitable Monsieur';
pauvre honteux: 'Man ashamed of his poverty'.

72. *Dieu . . . encore*: 'God bless you – And the good God bless you again'.

73. *c'est un cheval . . . monde*: 'It's the most stubborn horse in the world';
Peste: Literally 'Plague!';
mal a propos: 'Out of place'.

74. *once doublets*: A pair of ones in dice (i.e., the lowest score).

75. *cast*: Throw or stroke of fortune.

76. *the third—*: As Keymer points out, a third term might be *Bougre!* or *Foutre!* (as used to encourage two stubborn mules in *TS*, VII.xxv, pp. 420–21).

77. *Sancho's lamentation for his*: Reference to Sancho's lament following the theft of his ass (*Don Quixote*, Part I.xxiii).

78. *pannel*: Cloth placed under a saddle.

79. *St. Iago in Spain*: The shrine of St James in Santiago de Compostela (northwest Spain) – an important place of pilgrimage.

80. *eat the same bread . . . friend*: Paraphrase of 2 Samuel 12:3: 'the poor *man* had nothing, save one little ewe lamb, which . . . did eat of his own meat, and drank of his own cup, and lay in his bosom, and was unto him as a daughter' (see also n. 95 and n. 98 to vol. II).

81. *pavè*: 'Paving'.

82. *The thirstiest soul . . . cold water*: Cf. Proverbs 25:25: '*As* cold waters to a thirsty soul, so *is* good news from a far country'.

83. *clue*: Thread.

84. *though I cannot dry up . . . fairest of women*: Perhaps alluding to Isaiah 25:8: 'the Lord God will wipe away tears from off all faces'. Sterne paraphrases this text in sermons 10 and 15 (*Sermons*, pp. 102 and 147); in *The Journal to Eliza* he wishes to 'not only wipe away [Eliza's] tears but dry up the Sourse of them for ever' (*Letters*, p. 386).

85. *hôtel*: Large town house or mansion; 'hôtel' and 'hotel' are also used in *SJ* in the now common sense of a travellers' lodging (which usage became familiar in English during the 1760s).

86. *prevenancy*: Willingness to oblige, charm.

87. *maitre d'hotel*: Steward of a town house (also the master of a hotel for travellers – see n. 85 above).

88. *au desespoire*: 'In despair'.

89. *en egards vis a vis d'une femme*: 'With regards to a woman'.

90. *Quelle etourderie*: 'What thoughtlessness/carelessness!'

91. *par hazard*: 'By chance';
faux pas: 'Mistake'.

92. *Le Diable l'emporte*: 'The devil take it!'

93. *La voila*: 'There it is!'

94. *Je suis penetré . . . tout a vous*: 'I am filled with the deepest sadness and at the same time reduced to despair by this unforeseen return of the Corporal, which renders our meeting tonight the most impossible thing in the world. But let there be joy! And all of my joy will be in thinking of you. Love is *nothing* without sentiment. And sentiment is even *less* without love. It is said that one should never despair. It is also said that Monsieur le Corporal will be mounting guard on Wednesday: then it will be my turn. *Everyone has his turn.* While we wait – Long live love! And long live sweet nothings! I am, Madame, with all the most respectful and tender sentiments, all yours.' The drummer's letter echoes one of Sterne's – in 1765 he wrote of his own amorous career: 'I carry on my affairs quite in the French way, sentimentally—"*l'amour*" (say they) "*n'est rien sans sentiment*"' (*Letters*, p. 256).

95. *cabinet*: Centre of power or fashion (also a private apartment or chamber).

96. *Me voici! mes enfans*: 'Here I am! my children'.

97. *running at the ring of pleasure . . . love*: Images of a chivalric sport exploited by Sterne for bawdy innuendo (see Introduction, p. xxix).

98. *Alas, poor Yorick*: *Hamlet*, V.i.172.

99. *tourniquet*: Turnstile;
flambeau: Torch.

100. *grisset*: Young woman, particularly one working in a shop (and so-called because of the typically grey clothes of shop-workers). The term can suggest a girl of loose sexual morals.

101. *buckle*: Curl of hair.

102. *mais prenez guarde*: 'But be careful'.

103. *if tones and manners . . . shut them out*: The legibility of the body and the body's reliability as an index of meaning/character/the soul was a recurrent subject for Sterne (cf. especially *TS*, I.xxiii, pp. 59–60; III.iv, p. 132; IX.xiii, p. 517; and *Sermons*, p. 402).

104. *Attendez*: 'Wait!'

105. *Eugenius*: Usually regarded as a reference to the libertine and wit John Hall-Stevenson (1718–85), one of Sterne's closest friends. Eugenius appears often in *TS* as a faithful friend and adviser. Substantiating the identification, Sterne's daughter urged Hall to contribute to a biography of Sterne stressing ''twill prove that Eugenius was the friend of Yorick' (*Letters*, p. 453).

106. *thrum night-cap*: Cap made from coarse, waste threads.

107. *salique*: Observant of the Salic law excluding women from succession to the throne.

108. *surely man . . . sit alone*: Cf. Genesis 2:18: 'God said, *It is* not good that the man should be alone; I will make him an help meet for him.'

109. *reins*: The seat of the feelings or affections (literally 'kidneys').

110. *M'en croyez capable*: 'Do you think I'm capable of it?'

111. *Captain Tobias Shandy*: Uncle Toby, the good-natured and benevolent ex-soldier of *TS*.

112. *shagreen*: Untanned leather, often dyed green.

113. *Martini's concert at Milan*: Probably referring to Giovanni Battista Martini (1706–84), Italian priest, composer and famous theorist and teacher of music.

114. *chichesbee*: Form of '*cicisbeo*', the gallant of a married woman in Italy (a role Yorick apparently attempts to take on here).

115. *St. Cecilia*: Patron saint of music.

116. *who that was*: Another reference to Smollett, whose remarks on the deforming consequences of swaddling (*Travels*, letter xxx) are satirized later in the chapter.

117. *Mr. Shandy the elder*: Walter Shandy, father of Tristram and thwarted perfectionist in matters of childbirth and rearing. As Yorick observes, Walter Shandy is himself 'very short' (*TS*, VI.xviii, p. 363).

118. *esplanade*: Open space.

119. *A poor defenceless being . . . posture*: An incident adapted from Paul Scarron's picaresque novel *Roman comique* (1651), II.xvii (known to Sterne from *The Whole Comical Works of Monsʳ Scarron*, translated by Thomas Brown et al. and first published in 1700).

120. *queue*: Pigtail.

121. *centinel*: Sentry.

122. *bon mot*: 'Witty remark'.

123. *Haussez les mains, Monsieur l'Abbe*: 'Raise your hands, Father'.

124. *loges*: 'Boxes';
perdu: 'Hidden'.

125. *Quelle grossierte*: 'What rudeness!'

126. *Le pour, et le contre se trouvent en chaque nation*: 'The good and the bad are found in every nation'.

127. *sçavoir vivre*: 'social know-how'.

128. *Madame de Rambouliet*: Perhaps playfully recalling Catherine de Vivonne (1588–1665), Marquise de Rambouillet, a leading *précieuse* (see n. 5 above) whose salon was celebrated as a centre of fashionable manners and politeness.

129. *Rien que pisser*: 'Nothing but to piss'. The holograph manuscript of volume I (Egerton MS. 1610, in the British Library) shows that Sterne originally wrote the phrase in English but then rejected it in favour of the (pseudo-decorous) French.

130. *pluck your rose*: Euphemism for urination, as in Jonathan Swift's 'Strephon

and Chloe': 'None ever saw her pluck a Rose./Her dearest Comrades never caught her/Squat on her Hams, to make Maid's Water' (ll. 16–18).

131. *the chaste Castalia*: Greek nymph who escaped Apollo's advances by jumping into a spring on Mount Parnassos. The sacred 'Castalian Spring' was visited by pilgrims and its water used for cleansing the temple of the oracle at Delphi.

Notes to Volume II

1. *Polonius's advice to his son*: See *Hamlet*, I.iii.55–81.

2. *Comment*: 'How is that?/What?'.

3. *Count de B*****: Veiled depiction of Claude de Thiard (1721–1820), Comte de Bissy, distinguished general, academic and anglophile, who, it seems, helped Sterne to obtain a passport during his first trip to Paris in 1762 (see Cash, *LY*, pp. 128–9).

4. *C'est un Esprit fort*: 'He's a sharp wit/intellectual'.

5. *Les Egarments du Cœur & de l'Esprit*: Novel by Claude-Prosper Jolyot de Crébillon, known as Crébillon Fils (1707–77); it was translated as *The Wanderings of the Heart and Mind* (1751) and was branded as licentious. Sterne socialized with Crébillon in Paris in 1762 (see Cash, *LY*, pp. 136–7).

6. *Le Dieu m'en guard*: 'God protect me!'

7. *En verite, Monsieur, je mettrai cet argent apart*: 'In truth, Sir, I will save this money'.

8. *war with France*: When Sterne travelled to France in January 1762, the Seven Years War was still officially ongoing (to be ended by the Treaty of Paris in February 1763). Unlike Yorick, Sterne was not oblivious to the war but he did travel without a passport until obtaining one in Paris (see Cash, *LY*, pp. 116–29).

9. *apparament*: 'Obviously';
certes: 'Surely';
au moins: 'At least';
Cela n'empeche pas: 'That doesn't prevent it'.

10. *Pardi ... extraordinaires*: 'Of course! ... these English gentlemen are very extraordinary people'.

11. *Disguise thyself ... on that account*: Cf. Sterne's sermon 10: 'Consider slavery——what it is,——how bitter a draught, and how many millions have been made to drink of it' (*Sermons*, p. 99). In 1766, Ignatius Sancho, a freed African slave, wrote to Sterne quoting and praising this passage of the sermon. He urged Sterne to address the issue further, believing Sterne's writing might 'ease the Yoke of many' (*Letters*, pp. 282–3). Sterne replied expressing further

sympathy for the enslaved and pledging not to forget Sancho's letter (*Letters*, pp. 286–7). The passages here might be seen as a response to Sancho's plea.

12. *chymic*: I.e. alchemistic.

13. *I begun to figure . . . slavery*: Cf. sermon 10: 'Millions of our fellow-creatures, born to no inheritance but poverty and trouble . . .' (*Sermons*, p. 101); and cf. a passage in Sancho's letter: 'think in me, you behold the uplifted hands of Millions of my moorish brethren—Grief (you pathetically observe) is eloquent—figure to yourselves their attitudes—hear their supplicatory address—humanity must comply' (*Letters*, p. 283; and see n. 11 to vol. II).

14. *sickness of the heart . . . hope deferr'd*: Echoing Proverbs 13:12: 'Hope deferred maketh the heart sick.'

15. *I heard his chains . . . enter into his soul*: Alluding to and quoting Psalms 105:18 (The Book of Common Prayer), where Joseph's 'feet they hurt in the stocks: the iron entered into his soul'.

16. *Monsieur Le Duke de Choiseul*: César-Gabriel de Choiseul (1712–85), Minister for Foreign Affairs 1761–6, to whom Sterne applied for a passport.

17. *crest to my arms*: Yorick's coat of arms makes subtle reference to Sterne's own family heraldry and plays upon connections between his name and dialect forms of 'starling': 'starnel', 'starn' and even 'sterne' (see Michael J. O'Shea, 'Laurence Sterne's Displays of Heraldry', *The Shandean* 3 (1991), pp. 61–9).

18. *succours*: Means of protection.

19. *C'est une autre affaire*: 'That's another matter'.

20. *Le Patisser*: *Pâtissier* (pastry-seller).

21. *Chevalier de St. Louis*: Member of the Order of St Louis, established by Louis XIV in 1693 to reward distinguished Catholic soldiers; *patès*: 'Pastries/pies'.

22. *propreté*: 'Cleanliness'.

23. *the last peace*: The Treaty of Aix-la-Chapelle, which ended the War of the Austrian Succession in 1748.

24. *mounting*: Soldier's equipment; or the general expenses of maintaining a reputable military position.

25. *Rennes*: Capital and seat of the parliament of Brittany.

26. *Monsieur Le Count . . . tumbling them over*: Cf. Sterne's meeting in 1762, described in a letter to Garrick: ''Twas an odd incident when I was introduced to the Count de Bissie, which I was at his desire—I found him reading Tristram—' (*Letters*, p. 151).

27. *et ayez la bontè . . . honneur la*: 'And have the goodness, my dear friend . . . to do me that honour'.

28. *to spy the nakedness of the land*: Cf. Genesis 42:9, where Joseph says to his brethren 'Ye *are* spies; to see the nakedness of the land ye are come.'

29. *Ne craignez rien*: 'Fear nothing'.

30. *C'est bien dit*: 'It's well said'.

31. *Hèh bien! Monsieur l'Anglois*: 'Well! My English Sir'; *ni encore*: 'Nor moreover'.

32. *to spy the nakedness ... am I come*: See n. 28 to vol. II. Cf. Tristram expounding upon the ease a biographer would enjoy if '*Momus*'s glass' had been fixed in the human breast, allowing a view of 'the soul stark naked ...' (*TS*, I.xxiii, pp. 59–60).

33. *I have not seen the Palais royal ... Louvre*: Yorick eschews the usual attractions of the eighteenth-century tourist trail, unlike Smollett, who 'could not leave Paris, without carrying my wife and the girls to see the most remarkable places in and about this capital, such as the Luxemburg, the Palais-Royal, the Thuilleries, the Louvre ...' (*Travels*, letter vi).

34. *a temple, and would rather enter in*: Suggestively lewd allusion to biblical images of the body as a temple (see John 2:21; 1 Corinthians 3:16–17, 6:19; 2 Corinthians 6:16).

35. *transfiguration of Raphael itself*: Renowned painting at the church of San Pietro in Montorio – the historian Edward Gibbon declared in 1764 that it was 'esteemed the first picture in Rome and perhaps in the world'. 'You need not doubt', wrote Smollett, 'but that I went ... to view the celebrated transfiguration' (*Travels*, letter xxxiii).

36. *'tis a quiet journey ... better than we do*: Paraphrased from a letter explaining Sterne's 'design' in *SJ* 'to teach us to love the world and our fellow creatures better than we do—so it runs most upon those gentler passions and affections, which aid so much to it' (*Letters*, p. 401). As my introduction outlines, Sterne's letters do not reveal consistent intentions for the work.

37. *perplexing affair ... who I am*: Cf. Tristram's exchange with a French official: 'And who are you? said he.——Don't puzzle me; said I.' (*TS*, VII.xxxiii, p. 434).

38. *one of the first of our own church ... Denmark's jester*: Alluding to the criticism directed at Sterne when he published his *Sermons* under the pseudonym of Yorick (see Introduction, p. xv). The passage may be aimed specifically at the Bishop of Gloucester, William Warburton (1698–1779), who withdrew his early patronage of Sterne shortly after the *Sermons* appeared.

39. *Horwendillus's court ... he replied*: In the twelfth-century *Gesta Danorum* by Saxo Grammaticus (a source for Shakespeare's *Hamlet*), Horwendillus is Hamlet's (Amleth's) father. Tristram refers to this work when describing Yorick's descent from 'the king's chief Jester ... *Hamlet*'s Yorick' (*TS*, I.xi, pp. 21–2). Shakespeare's Hamlet, when confronted with Yorick's skull, reflects upon Alexander the Great's mortality and the levelling power of death (*Hamlet*,

V.i.184–98) – perhaps the point of the Count's reply. 'Alexander the copper-smith' appears in Timothy 4:14.

40. *Et Monsieur . . . Vous etes Yorick*: 'And, Sir, is it Yorick? . . . – I am he . . . – You? – Me – I who have the honour of speaking with you . . . – You are Yorick.'

41. *elysian fields . . . dishonours*: Cf. Virgil, *The Aenied*, VI.450–76, where the Trojan hero Aeneas travels through Hades and re-encounters Dido, the queen of Carthage who killed herself when abandoned by Aeneas.

42. *Surely this is not walking . . . in vain*: Cf. Psalm 39:6: 'Surely every man walketh in a vain show: surely they are disquieted in vain.'

43. *Un homme qui rit . . . dangereuz*: 'A man who laughs . . . will never be dangerous'; *Et vous plaisantez*: 'And do you jest?'

44. *the last we had . . . Charles IId*: Probably referring to the royalist actor and dramatist Thomas Killigrew (1612–83), appointed Master of the Revels in 1673.

45. *patriots*: A term often used with irony to describe self-interested individuals whose ambitions were veiled beneath a professed love of country.

46. *Voila un persiflage*: 'There's an irony!'

47. *Bevoriskius*: Latinized name of Johan van Beverwijck (1594–1647), Dutch physician and medical writer.

48. *Mais passe, pour cela*: Ambiguous phrase probably meaning 'Never mind that' (i.e. the Count tells Yorick to forget about such urbanities as it is implied he has uttered);
Vraiment . . . Les François sont polis: 'Really . . . the French are polite'.

49. *politesse de cœur*: 'Politeness of heart'.

50. *too serious*: Cf. Tristram's comment on the French: 'The devil take the serious character of these people! quoth I—(aside) they understand no more of IRONY than this——' (*TS*, VII.xxxiv, p. 435).

51. *Mais vous plaisantez*: 'But you're joking'.

52. *band-box*: Light box for holding ribbons, caps, millinery etc.

53. *merchande de modes*: 'Fashion seller/milliner'.

54. *hussive*: Roll of cloth for holding needles, cotton etc.

55. *thou hast made us—and not we ourselves*: Adapted from Psalms 100:3: 'the Lord he *is* God: *it is* he *that* hath made us, and not we ourselves'.

56. *Voyez vous, Monsieur*: 'Look, Sir'.

57. *et tout cela*: 'And all that';
en conscience: 'In good faith'.

58. *cullibility*: Gullibility.

59. *C'est deroger à noblesse*: 'That is to depart from nobility' (specifically, to lose the privileges of nobility by practising a 'low' profession – like the 'Chevalier de St. Louis'). The literal meaning of *déroger* – 'to lower oneself' – is echoed in La Fleur's bow.

60. *Et encore*: 'And moreover'.

61. *both the Indies*: The East Indies and the West Indies – regarded from a European perspective as immensely valuable assets (and fought over by England and France during the Seven Years War).

62. *king of Babylon . . . interpretation*: In Daniel 2:1–11, Nebuchadnezzar, King of Babylon, commands the Chaldeans to interpret his dream (which he has forgotten).

63. *pour s'adoniser*: 'To beautify himself' (derived from Adonis, the attractive youth of classical mythology, the verb was typically used playfully/ironically).

64. *friperie*: 'Second-hand clothing' (Paris contained both a Rue de la Grande Friperie and a Rue de la Petite Friperie).

65. *bag and a solitaire*: Pouch for holding the back of a wig, and a loose necktie.

66. *fripier*: 'second-hand clothes dealer';
bien brodées: 'well embroidered'.

67. *pour faire le galant vis à vis de sa maitresse*: 'To play the gallant to his mistress'/'to court his mistress'.

68. *in the midst of the house of bondage*: Common biblical image of Israel's captivity.

69. *Behold!—Behold, I am thy servant*: Compound of common biblical expressions (see, for example, 1 Kings 18:36; 2 Kings 16:7).

70. *traiteur*: 'Caterer'/'restaurateur'.

71. *Rabelais's time*: François Rabelais (1483/94?–1553), French cleric, scholar and author of the satirical *Gargantua and Pantagruel* (1532–64; trans. 1653–94); much admired and emulated by Sterne, particularly in *TS*.

72. *as ever Gruter or Jacob Spon did upon a nonsensical inscription*: Jan Gruytère (1560–1627), Dutch historian and writer on classical inscriptions; Jacob Spon (1647–85), French antiquarian.

73. *garde d'eau*: 'Beware water', a warning cry shouted from windows before throwing slops and refuse into the street.

74. *a gascon*: A native of Gascony; proverbially a boaster (from the reputation of the Gascon people for immodest self-importance);
harquebuss: Heavy portable gun.

75. *castor*: Fur hat.

76. *fauxbourgs*: Inner suburbs.

77. *pontific*: Pertaining to a bridge (a facetious usage); given that 'the thunder of the church' has caused much of the notary's distress, the more typical meaning – 'pertaining to a pontiff' or 'papal' – is also wittily recalled.

78. *bandoleer*: Broad belt worn over the shoulder, used for holding ammunition.

79. *that Book . . . acquitted*: Probably a reference to the 'book of life' in Revelation

20:12, '[the] book was opened, which is *the book* of life: and the dead were judged out of those things which were written'.

80. *Juste ciel*: 'Good heavens!';
gage d'amour: 'token of love'.

81. *Capadosia . . . Bible*: Cf. Acts 2:9–10: '. . . in Judaea, and Cappadocia, in Pontus, and Asia, Phrygia, and Pamphylia . . .' (Sterne also seems to draw upon this text's effusion of proper names in *TS*, VI.xxx, p. 378).

82. *concentre*: Concentrate.

83. *Cour d'amour*: 'Court of love'.

84. *Mons. P*****'s concerts upon any other terms*: The farmers-general (*fermiers généraux*) paid the treasury a fixed sum for the privilege of collecting provincial taxes with entitlement to the profits. Huge wealth was amassed by many, such as Alexandre-Jean-Joseph Le Riche de la Popelinière (1692–1762), whose identity is suggested here. Sterne met Popelinière in 1762 and was invited to one of his lavish concerts (see *Letters*, p. 155; Cash, *LY*, p. 132).

85. *esprit*: Wit or free-thinker.

86. *deist—then devôte*: 'Deist' (and 'deism') carried eclectic meanings: generally, it suggested one with a belief in a supreme being but a distrust of orthodox revealed religion, but it was also applied to varieties of free-thinkers, including atheists. A *devôte* is a woman ostentatiously displaying her observance of institutional religion.

87. *Mons. D*** . . . said against it*: The monumental Enlightenment reference work *L'Encyclopédie; ou, Dictionnaire raisonné des sciences, des arts, et des métiers* (1751–80) was notorious for the rational scepticism of many of its articles and for its attacks against established religion. Mons. D*** suggests its chief editor, Denis Diderot (1713–84), the philosopher, dramatist, novelist and critic, with whom Sterne became friendly in Paris (see Cash, *LY*, pp. 138–9). Abbe M*** suggests André Morellet (1727–1819), who contributed articles on political economy, theology and metaphysics to the *Encyclopédie*.

88. *Count de Faineant*: Name suggesting an idler, a sluggard.

89. *plus badinant*: 'More jaunty'.

90. *Pardi! . . . enfant*: 'Of course! This Mr Yorick has just as much wit as the rest of us. — He reasons well, . . . – He's a good fellow.'

91. *poor Maria . . . Moulines*: See *TS*, IX.xxiv. pp. 528–30. The pathos of the Maria episodes in both works was greatly admired by many early readers and the character became something of a sentimental icon. Maria appeared in numerous spin-offs: the episodes were reproduced in *The Beauties of Sterne* (1782) and in *Sterne's Maria; A Pathetic Story* (containing a spurious continuation of her story); she was painted by Joseph Wright of Derby and Angelica Kauffmann; she appeared in engravings; she was the subject of an opera and of several songs and ballads.

92. *Knight of the Woeful Countenance*: Name given to Don Quixote by Sancho Panza (*Don Quixote*, Part I.xix).

93. *Her goat ... said she*: Parodic reworking of Andrew Marvell's lyric poem 'Nymph Complaining for the Death of Her Faun'. The work of Marvell (1621–78) was not widely known at the time but was admired by several in Sterne's circle, so the parody may have been included for this select group of readers (see Tom Keymer, 'Marvell, Thomas Hollis, and Sterne's Maria: Parody in *A Sentimental Journey*', *The Shandean* 5 (1993), pp. 9–31).

94. *God tempers the wind .. shorn lamb*: Translation of a French proverb, '*Dieu mesure le froid à la brebis tondue*'.

95. *eat ... cup*: Paraphrased from 2 Samuel 12:3 (see n. 80 to vol. I and n. 98 below).

96. *incense ... accepted*: Compound of biblical expressions (see, for example, Isaiah 56:7; Deuteronomy 33:10).

97. *I hate salutations and greetings in the market-place*: In contrast to the scribes of Mark 12:38 who '*love* salutations in the marketplaces'.

98. *eat... daughter*: Paraphrased from 2 Samuel 12:3 (see n. 80 to vol. I and n. 95 to vol. II).

99. *imbibe the oil and wine ... for ever*: Another allusion to the good Samaritan (Luke 10:33–34, and see n. 39 to vol. I).

100. *thy divinity ... within me [...] my soul ... destruction*: Paraphrased from Joseph Addison, *Cato* (1713), V.i.5–7.

101. *if a hair of our head but falls on the ground*: Suggestive of various biblical passages (1 Samuel 14:45; 2 Samuel 14:11; 1 Kings 1:52; Matthew 10:29–30; Luke 12:7).

102. *Eugenius draws my curtain*: Cf. Eugenius (see n. 105 to vol. I) 'drawing *Yorick*'s curtain' in *TS*, I.xii, p. 12.

103. *thill-horse*: Horse between the thills, or shafts, of a carriage.

104. *potagerie*: 'Kitchen garden'.

105. *sabots*: Clogs.

106. *vielle*: Hurdy-gurdy.

107. *It was not till the middle ... could pay*: Cf. sermon 20's depiction of religion underlying festivity (*Sermons*, pp. 190–91); and Tristram's dance with the peasants of Languedoc: 'Just disposer of our joys and sorrows, cried I, why could not a man sit down in the lap of content here—and dance, and sing, and say his prayers, and go to heaven with this nut brown maid?' (*TS*, VII.xliii, p. 445).

108. *The Case of Delicacy*: Given the suggested indelicacy of the chapter's conclusion, Sterne may have intended a subtle innuendo here: 'case' was an old slang term for 'vagina', and it retained some eighteenth-century currency, as in John Wilkes' notoriously obscene 'Essay on Woman' (1763): 'His Pego measur'd to the Female Case,/Betwixt a Woman's Thighs his proper Place'.

109. *Voiturin*: Coach driver.

110. *servant-maid*: The events that follow seem to be based upon an anecdote told to Sterne by John Crauford of Errol, a witty Scot whom Sterne met in Paris in 1765 (se Cash, *LY*, pp. 230–31). Sterne's version intensifies the erotic suggestiveness of the original.

111. *corking pins*: Large pins.

112. *I leave to the reader . . . first complaint*: Playfully transferring to the reader the responsibility for any indelicate interpretation was a favourite device for Sterne. Cf., for example, Tristram's declaration that his writing's decency depends 'upon the cleanliness of my reader's imaginations' (*TS*, III.xxxi, p. 178). Sterne wrote of *SJ*: 'If it is not thought a chaste book, mercy on them that read it, for they must have warm imaginations indeed!' (*Letters*, p. 403). The possible innuendo in 'Case' (see n. 108 to vol. II) is perhaps here recalled in 'fault'.

113. *the Fille de Chambre's . . .* END OF VOL. II: Without concluding punctuation, Sterne's final sentence suggestively continues into the volume marker. Many later editions changed the nature of the ambiguity with a concluding dash: 'the Fille de Chambre's—'.

PENGUIN CLASSICS

THE LIFE AND OPINIONS OF TRISTRAM SHANDY, GENTLEMAN   LAURENCE STERNE

'L—d! said my mother, what is all this story about? –
A COCK and a BULL, said Yorick – and one of the best of its kind I
ever heard'

Laurence Sterne's great masterpiece of bawdy humour and rich satire
defies any attempt to categorize it. Part novel, part digression, its
gloriously disordered narrative interweaves the birth and life of the
unfortunate 'hero' Tristram Shandy, the eccentric philosophy of his
father Walter, the amours and military obsessions of Uncle Toby, and
a host of other characters, including Dr Slop, Corporal Trim and the
parson Yorick. A joyful celebration of the endless possibilities of the art
of fiction, *Tristram Shandy* is also a wry demonstration of its limitations.

The text and notes of this volume are based on the acclaimed Florida
Edition, with a critical introduction by Melvyn New and Christopher
Ricks's introductory essay from the first Penguin Classics edition of
the novel.

'The excellent Florida *Tristram Shandy* . . . will be the definitive edition'
Studies in English Literature

'The book that I would never tire of . . . Sterne was about 250 years ahead
of his time' Roy Porter

THE FLORIDA EDITION
Edited by Melvyn New and Joan New

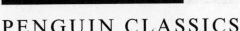
PENGUIN CLASSICS

GULLIVER'S TRAVELS   JONATHAN SWIFT

'I felt something alive moving on my left Leg ... when bending my Eyes downwards as much as I could, I perceived it to be a human Creature not six Inches high'

Shipwrecked and cast adrift, Lemuel Gulliver wakes to find himself on Lilliput, an island inhabited by little people, whose height makes their quarrels over fashion and fame seem ridiculous. His subsequent encounters – with the crude giants of Brobdingnag, the philosophical Houyhnhnms and brutish Yahoos – give Gulliver new, bitter insights into human behaviour. Swift's savage satire views mankind in a distorted hall of mirrors as a diminished, magnified and finally bestial species, presenting us with an uncompromising reflection of ourselves.

This text, based on the first edition of 1726, reproduces all its original illustrations and includes an introduction by Robert Demaria, Jr., which discusses the ways *Gulliver's Travels* has been interpreted since its first publication.

'A masterwork of irony ... that contains both a dark and bitter meaning and a joyous, extraordinary creativity of imagination. That is why it has lived for so long' Malcolm Bradbury

Edited with an introduction by Robert DeMaria, Jr

PENGUIN CLASSICS

CHRONICLES OF THE CANONGATE
WALTER SCOTT

The Highland Widow / The Two Drovers / The Surgeon's Daughter

'Go, disown the royal Stuart, for whom your father, and his fathers, and your mother's fathers, have crimsoned many a field with their blood'

Ranging from the wilds of the Scottish Highlands to the dusty streets of Madras, these three masterly stories all show lives transformed – and, in some cases, destroyed – by worlds and cultures in conflict. In 'The Highland Widow', a mother is devastated when her son announces his intention to join the British army to fight in America, and uses all her cunning to keep him at home. 'The Two Drovers' is a tale of a prophecy fulfilled in which the Englishman Harry Wakefield is set against his Scottish friend Robin Oid in a destructive and ultimately tragic quarrel. 'The Surgeon's Daughter' follows the fortunes of three young Scots who attempt to settle in India during the early years of the British Empire.

Based on the authoritative Edinburgh edition, which follows the text of the Scott collection in its original form, this edition features a new introduction by Claire Lamont. It also includes a chronology of Scott's life and works, textual and historical notes and a glossary.

Edited with an introduction by Claire Lamont

PENGUIN CLASSICS

AGNES GREY   ANNE BRONTË

'The name of governess, I soon found, was a mere mockery ... my pupils had no more notion of obedience than a wild, unbroken colt'

When her family becomes impoverished after a disastrous financial speculation, Agnes Grey determines to find work as a governess in order to contribute to their meagre income and assert her independence. But Agnes's enthusiasm is swiftly extinguished as she struggles first with the unmanageable Bloomfield children and then with the painful disdain of the haughty Murray family; the only kindness she receives comes from Mr Weston, the sober young curate. Drawing on her own experience, Anne Brontë's first novel offers a compelling personal perspective on the desperate position of unmarried, educated women for whom becoming a governess was the only respectable career open in Victorian society.

This edition also includes Charlotte Brontë's memoir of her sisters, the 'Biographical Notice of Ellis and Acton Bell'. Angeline Goreau examines Anne Brontë's complex relationship with her sisters and her unhappy career as a governess as influences in writing Agnes Grey.

'Amazingly modern ... Agnes Grey is a little masterpiece'
Victoria Glendinning, *Daily Telegraph*

Edited with an introduction and notes by Angeline Goreau

THE STORY OF PENGUIN CLASSICS

Before 1946 ...'Classics' are mainly the domain of academics and students, without readable editions for everyone else. This all changes when a little-known classicist, E. V. Rieu, presents Penguin founder Allen Lane with the translation of Homer's *Odyssey* that he has been working on and reading to his wife Nelly in his spare time.

1946 *The Odyssey* becomes the first Penguin Classic published, and promptly sells three million copies. Suddenly, classic books are no longer for the privileged few.

1950s Rieu, now series editor, turns to professional writers for the best modern, readable translations, including Dorothy L. Sayers's *Inferno* and Robert Graves's *The Twelve Caesars*, which revives the salacious original.

1960s The Classics are given the distinctive black jackets that have remained a constant throughout the series's various looks. Rieu retires in 1964, hailing the Penguin Classics list as 'the greatest educative force of the 20th century'.

1970s A new generation of translators arrives to swell the Penguin Classics ranks, and the list grows to encompass more philosophy, religion, science, history and politics.

1980s The Penguin American Library joins the Classics stable, with titles such as *The Last of the Mohicans* safeguarded. Penguin Classics now offers the most comprehensive library of world literature available.

1990s The launch of Penguin Audiobooks brings the classics to a listening audience for the first time, and in 1999 the launch of the Penguin Classics website takes them online to a larger global readership than ever before.

The 21st Century Penguin Classics are rejacketed for the first time in nearly twenty years. This world famous series now consists of more than 1300 titles, making the widest range of the best books ever written available to millions – and constantly redefining the meaning of what makes a 'classic'.

The Odyssey continues ...

The best books ever written

PENGUIN (🐧) CLASSICS

SINCE 1946

Find out more at www.penguinclassics.com